The Priestess and the Yōkai

Book II

Lindsey Merril

Chapter 1

Eiji held a folded scroll in her hands. A messenger from the western castle had brought it that morning. She looked at the neat kanji that spelled out her name for the twentieth time. Sesshoshi's writing. His request. Eiji was to attend a banquet at the western castle in three days time and supervise Lord Ko for the evening.

Eiji knew this was an honour. If her relationship with Lord Ko was unwelcome she would never have received the invitation. And it was a rare chance to enter the western castle and be among the most powerful yōkai in all of Edo... but, she would have to see Lord Sesshoshi once again.

Eiji's heart pounded in her chest at the thought. Her cheeks grew warm.

As the scroll instructed, she would stay the night in the western castle's guest wing. Lord Sesshoshi would escort her back home the next day. Eiji put the letter down. It was crinkled now. She wasn't ready to see Sesshoshi again, not after the time they'd spent together in the world where fairytales lived.

Where all that had ever been created or partially created had a living, physical form.

Where she'd fallen in love with him.

Was it a mistake to erase his memories of me? Eiji thought. She remembered the feel of it, the silky moon robe that she'd stolen from the Tale of the Bamboo Cutter. In the story, the moon king had used it to erase Princess Kaguya's memory of her time on earth. Eiji hadn't even known if it would work when she placed it on Sesshoshi's shoulders.

It had.

The moon robe was gone now. It disintegrated shortly after it touched Sesshoshi's shoulders. She'd thought it would be best for him to forget and for her to move on, but Eiji couldn't move on.

She still remembered his warmth. His touch.

Before Sesshoshi began making appearances in her village, Eiji had felt listless and lost. He changed that and she'd thrown it away. For what? In some ways she couldn't remember, but then again the truth stared her right in the face everyday. Every time yōkai killed or abused humans. Every time humans cursed yōkai.

She sighed and went to inform her father that she would be away for a few days.

Sesshoshi's letter brought other questions to her mind. *Did he remember? No. It's not possible.* Though Eiji didn't exactly know how the powers of the moon robe would work in her world. How could she be sure? Why had Sesshoshi written her and not Lord Ko's father, Lord Jou?

Eiji found her father working in their herb garden and told him her news.

"You're going to the western castle? To be among yōkai?" Hiroki said. He rubbed his head, brows creased with worry. "We can't deny their request... but I'm not too happy to send my only child into a place teaming with yōkai."

"I know, father." Eiji patted his shoulder. Her mother died while giving birth to Eiji. She knew her father was afraid of losing her as well. "I'll be careful. I'll be with Lord Ko most of the time and I'll be under Lord Jou's protection."

Hiroki nodded. "I suppose so. When do you have to leave?"

"The banquet is in three days. I should leave tomorrow morning."

"Alright," Hiroki huffed.

Eiji bowed to her father and then went to pack. She found her finest kimono and held it out in front of her. It would look like a dirty rag next to the kimonos of the female yōkai visiting the castle, but it was all she had. Eiji packed a few provisions as well.

It was late and she still wanted to bathe. Eiji threw the rest of her belongings in a pile. Then she rifled through her grandmother's scrolls, looking for a fairytale to take with her. She went through them one by one. She loved feeling the texture of the paper. *I don't spend enough time with all of you anymore.* Eiji silently laughed at herself. When she uncurled The Snow Woman and a small piece of writing fell out. Cold panic shot down her body as Eiji thought she'd ripped the scroll. She hadn't. It was a separate sheet. Eiji scanned its contents. It was definitely written by her grandmother. Eiji would know her hand writing anywhere. The message was short, some kind of story about Tsuru herself and how she lived in the fairytale world. Eiji smiled.

She tucked the piece of writing back in with The Snow Woman's scroll. The Snow Woman wasn't the best story for children. Eiji chose The Adventures of Kintaro instead and placed it with her other belongings.

Eiji headed to the bath house. She expected Haruka would be there already. It was dark out now and there wouldn't be anyone else in the bath house except Haruka and herself. They chose to bathe late at night so the other villagers wouldn't bother them.

Eiji was the village priestess, but the townspeople kept their distance from her. She had a boy's name, which was odd to begin with, and her family had a reputation for being *strange*. Eiji didn't help by associating with both the yōkai Lords of the west. Her best friend, Haruka, was a half-breed. Haruka's mother was a badger yōkai and her father was human. That also got her a bit of attention.

Eiji pushed the blue cloth covering the doorway of the bath house aside. She was disappointed to find it empty. She must have missed Haruka. Eiji would have to tell her about the trip to the western castle when she returned. Eiji smiled, Haruka would be annoyed about that.

Eiji bathed quickly and then headed back to her home. She wanted to fall asleep as soon as possible to stop her mind from wandering to thoughts of Sesshoshi.

She missed him.

His hands on her body. The way he smelled. How his golden eyes looked at her when she spoke about something that

4

interested him.

Stop.

She closed her eyes and slept.

Eiji woke at dawn. She dressed in her priestess garb, a white hakui and red hakama. She wasn't sure if showing up at the western castle in her priestess robes was the best idea. Priestesses and yōkai were eternal enemies. Priestesses were the only ones who could kill yōkai by purifying them. But she owned no other clothing aside from her kimono, and she wasn't going to risk dirtying it on the road. Eiji secured her scythe attached to a long chain around her waist. Sesshoshi had taught her how to improve her technique with the scythe while they were in the Tale of the Bamboo Cutter. It had led to other... things.

Eiji's cheeks began to burn. She pushed the memories aside with force.

"Leaving already?" Hiroki asked.

She smiled at her father. "It's better to start early before it becomes too hot." She gathered her things and bowed to her father.

Eiji took off down the dusty village road. As she walked along the wide path leading out of Yamamachi, Eiji found it a bit annoying that transportation hadn't been arranged for her by Lord Jou. Eiji supposed that would be asking too much since she was just a *lowly* human. *Sesshoshi doesn't think of you that way,* she thought. *Not after...* Eiji stopped herself. He wouldn't remember anyway.

She should count her blessings. The western and southern lands were the only ones that tolerated humans. The northern and eastern lords culled their human populations. Those that were lucky enough to escape lived in various villages far from where they once called home. Eiji wondered if the Shogun planned on using the mysterious weapon, the one Sesshoshi had told her about, against those yōkai first.

The weapon. Eiji hadn't thought about it for a while. It had been what pushed Sesshoshi to visit her village and pick up

Lord Ko at the end of their days together. Eiji once wondered if it was the reason he forced himself to become interested in her.

No.

He told her several times that that was not the case. She believed him, which only made her heart hurt more. *What ever made you think you could get over him. You think about him all the time.* Eiji scolded herself.

It didn't take longer before it became hot and humid, but Eiji enjoyed the walk anyway. She drew stares and murmurs from those working close to the main roads. This kind of attention was different than what she was use to. Her village kept their distance from her and Eiji believed everyone would treat her with the same disregard or avoidance. But she found that the villagers she met on her journey were friendly and kind. Farmers waved to her from the rice fields. Children ran around her singing "Priestess! Priestess!" in joyous voices. *Is this what it's like to be a priestess in other villages?*

When it grew dark Eiji found an inn. She was able to trade a night's stay for providing some pain relief for the inn keeper's elderly mother. Eiji knelt next to the pale old woman. There was a pang in her chest. This woman reminded Eiji so much of her own grandmother. *What I would give to see her again.* Eiji missed her grandmother everyday.

Eiji placed her hands on the woman's stomach and let her reiki flow out. The old woman's body stopped straining and relaxed into the futon. The woman fell into a deep sleep. The inn keeper thanked Eiji and showed her to her room. It was small and clean. Simple in a way that Eiji enjoyed.

She lay on her futon and found she couldn't get up again. She would bathe in the morning and then continue walking for another full day, but for now she would rest. Her body ached and her eyes closed before she could try and stop them.

Eiji woke at dawn to start her journey once again. She bathed and dressed and headed back out on the main road.

In the silhouette of the sun rise she could see a large statue of a wolf yōkai towering over the castle. The western castle lay between the protective stance of the wolf's legs. Eiji remembered it was the statue of one of Sesshoshi's ancestor's, though she didn't know which one. It looked small from where she stood but Eiji knew an entire city sat between those paws. She had a long way to walk today.

She started out, determined to make it there before the worst heat of the day hit. It took her several hours and her feet throbbed, but finally Eiji arrived at the castle gates.

The yōkai that kept watch regarded her with suspicion. "What do you want, human?" The soldier had long white hair like Sesshoshi, though his was braided and hung down to his lower back.

Eiji said nothing. She presented her letter from Lord Sesshoshi to the castle guard. He grunted and moved aside. Eiji slipped inside the gates.

The castle was somewhere in the centre. It was surrounded by a village much larger than her own. It didn't take long before Eiji became lost in the crowds. She was surprised and relieved to see she wasn't the only human. Human merchants and peasants mingled with the tall, statuesque yōkai that roamed the grounds. Many of the merchants stalls and nearby homes were decorated with white and red linens and silks. *The western colours.*

Eiji started to feel like she was walking in circles when she bumped into someone and fell backwards. Eiji looked up to see a dark haired yōkai. His wavy hair cascaded down his back, over his armour and royal blue kimono.

Her breath caught in her throat as she stared wide eyed at Lord Ryuu, Lord of the North. *The human killer.* She'd know him anywhere.

Eiji jumped to her feet and bowed deeply. She hoped there were rules against killing humans while within the walls of the western castle. "My deepest apologies Lord Ryuu."

He eyed her for a moment. His lips curved downward. "Be more careful. I do not want your stench on me," he muttered and turned from her. Eiji glared at his retreating form, the anger rising up within her. Eiji knew he hated humans. His lands were one of the few that exterminated any human settlements on their territory. And still his words irked her. *I don't smell.* Eiji became aware of the way her clothes stuck to her sweaty body. *OK. Maybe I smell a little.*

She returned to her task of finding her way into the castle. Finally, she came upon a wide gate. More yōkai guards were posted out front. Eiji showed a tall, handsome yōkai her note from Lord Sesshoshi. He flashed her a toothy grin.

"I can escort you to our Lord Sesshoshi if you wish," the yōkai said in a smooth tone. Eiji eyed him. She recognized a flirt when she saw one, but she was lost.

"Yes, please."

"And you are?" He asked as he led the way. Eiji fell into step beside him.

"Eiji."

"I'm Arata," he grinned down at her. Arata chatted with her about idle topics as he led her down the lavish halls. All the shōji screens were plain yet elegant and the wood floors immaculate. Eiji felt out of place in her dusty clothes. The deeper inside the castle they went, the more nervous Eiji became.

She would see Sesshoshi again.

Very soon.

Arata brought her to a shōji screen with two western crests on it. She could feel Sesshoshi on the other side. His powerful aura was hard to ignore.

Arata was still chatting. Eiji wasn't use to yōkai being this openly kind and flirtatious towards humans. Is this what life was like in larger cities or was this just how Arata himself was?

"A woman as lovely as you should be seen on my arm tomorrow night," Arata grinned, flashing his elongated canines.

"Ah, but I can't forsake my duty to Lord Ko after an invitation from Lord Sesshoshi himself," Eiji said. She blushed as Arata took her hand and kissed the back of it. The shōji screen slid open with a snap. Eiji looked up to see Sesshoshi standing before them. Eiji's heart leapt to her throat. Arata dropped her

8

hand as if burned by reiki. He straightened. Both Eiji and Arata bowed respectfully to Sesshoshi.

"Arata, I believe you are done here," Sesshoshi said.

"Yes, Lord Sesshoshi," Arata said and bowed once again, leaving quickly. Sesshoshi watched him leave and turned to look at Eiji.

She looked into his golden eyes. She wasn't sure what she saw there. *Did he remember? No, there was no way his memories had returned.* Eiji repeated the thought until she was sure she believed it.

It was painful to see him standing there knowing she couldn't embrace him. He clenched his jaw. There was tension in his broad shoulders. Eiji recognized all the signs that he was annoyed. She just couldn't figure out why.

"Lord Sesshoshi. Thank you for the invitation. I'm honoured to watch Lord Ko during your family's banquet," Eiji said and bowed low once again.

"Hn."

He must not remember. He would have said something by now. It was permanent then. Eiji realized in that moment that she'd always held a small hope that he would regain his memories. Seeing his reaction to her now meant she had to once again come to terms with the fact that she was no one to him.

"I will show you to your quarters." Sesshoshi turned and led her down the hall.

When they rounded the corner Eiji saw Lord Ko at the end of the corridor. He spotted her too and squeaked. "Eiji!" He ran down the hall, though his guardian tried to grab him. In the blink of an eye Lord Ko was right in front of her and leaping into her arms. Eiji recoiled from the impact. She thanked her own good sense for teaching Lord Ko that humans were fragile compared to yōkai.

"Hello little Lord," Eiji said with a fond smile. She placed him on the ground and told him to scurry back to his guardian. "I'll see you tomorrow night."

"Yes, Eiji!"

Sesshoshi led her to her room. It was so beautiful that she was afraid to step inside. The tatami mats were pristine. The tapestries on the wall told beautiful stories of female yōkai that had lived in the past. Eiji followed each tale with her eyes. *Maybe these women live in the fairytale world too.*

"Thank you, Sesshoshi," Eiji said quietly.

"Lord Sesshoshi," he corrected.

"Forgive me, my Lord," Eiji said. Her response sounded hollow to her own ears. She mentally kicked herself for her mistake. She wasn't use to having to speak to him like this. They had become so familiar to one another in the fairytale world.

She turned to look at him. To double check. There was nothing in his eyes that told her he remembered. She was nothing but Lord Ko's human pet again.

Sesshoshi left her alone and Eiji was glad for it.

It was nearly dark. Eiji was exhausted from her full day of walking. She explored her room, moving the shōji screens around to discover her very own bath. Eiji had never had such a luxury before. Eiji undressed. She slipped into the hot water of the bath and sighed deeply. She could live in this bath forever. The warmth seeped into her bones and helped to lift her weariness.

Eiji stayed in the waters longer than she should. When she emerged from the tub she was dizzy from the heat. She readied for bed and rolled out her futon. Laying down felt heavenly. If she were Sesshoshi's mate she could enjoy these kinds of comforts every day. *Stop it.* But her mind continued to supply her with images of comfort and luxury until she drifted off to sleep.

The next morning Eiji woke just after dawn. She had slept well and felt refreshed. She dressed in her priestess garb and ventured out into the castle halls. On the road, Eiji had felt welcomed, but it was immediately clear that the atmosphere in the western castle would be very different. Yōkai eyed her everywhere she went. Yōkai from the north and east snarled at her. It was easy to tell them apart from the yōkai of the south and west due to the clothing they wore. Fashion varied a lot between both region and species.

"How could Lord Jou allow a human priestess in his home?"

"I heard it is because Lord Ko is fond of her."

"She smells."

Eiji frowned. She had bathed last night.

All the gossip and hostility made her feel like she was back at home in Yamamachi. The corridors were packed with servants and guests that milled about. Eiji focused on locating Sesshoshi's aura. She wasn't too keen on subjecting herself to him once again, but she needed to know what to do, if anything, before the banquet tonight.

She found his powerful aura at the far side of the castle and headed towards it.

Eiji tried her best to move through the halls quietly and without bumping into anyone. She didn't want to stand out more than she already did. She saw Sesshoshi up ahead. A red-headed female yōkai was speaking with him. No, flirting. She was flirting with him, though Sesshoshi didn't seem very interested.

Jealousy flared inside Eiji and her temper rose with it.

Sesshoshi turned his sharp gaze toward her.

Eiji's heart jumped into her throat.

He smirked at her.

That looks like the Sesshoshi I remember, Eiji thought. His mask fell back into place. The emotion disappeared so quickly Eiji wondered if she'd imagined it.

The female yōkai frowned when Eiji stopped in front of Lord Sesshoshi.

"My Lord. Sorry to interrupt, but I wanted to know if there was something I should be doing before the banquet tonight," Eiji said.

"No. There is nothing. I will escort you to Lord Ko at the hour of the dog," Sesshoshi said.

"Thank you, my Lord." Eiji bowed low and headed back towards her room.

She overheard the girl snickering. "How horrible Lord Sesshoshi, that you have to deal with that human."

"Hn."

Eiji walked faster down the hall. She turned several corners and realized she was completely lost. Yōkai brushed by her and she didn't feel she could ask any of them where the guest quarters were.

"You look like a little lost lamb," a voice said. Eiji turned. It was Arata.

"Arata! I *am* lost," Eiji laughed.

"Here. I'll walk you back to your quarters." Arata held out an arm to her. Eiji took it. She was happy to see a friendly face, but she wasn't sure she liked how Arata smiled at her. It was too nice, too sweet, but she wasn't going to say no to aid when she had no idea where her room was. Arata guided her through the halls, taking turn after turn. His guidance allowed her to look closer at the castle walls. The shōji screens weren't elaborately decorated like human castle's were rumoured to be. The screens were white with only some covered with the western family crest. *It'll be hard to find my way around when everything looks the same.*

Arata stopped in front of her door. "Here you are."

"How did you know this was my room?"

"Once we were in the guest wing I easily followed your scent." There was that too wide grin again.

"Oh, right. Thank you." Eiji bowed.

"No problem." Arata grinned at her. Eiji bid him farewell before he could say more. She slipped into her room and closed the shōji screen with a snap.

Eiji sunk to the floor. Only a few more hours until the party and then she would venture home, never to see Lord Sesshoshi again.

Chapter 2

Sesshoshi went to fetch Eiji before the party began. He had waited for this day since his father suggested Eiji watch Lord Ko during the banquet. Sesshoshi seconded the idea, saying it would look good for demon-human relations if Eiji was invited to the castle.

All he wanted was to see her again.

It had taken over a month, but slowly Sesshoshi remembered everything from their time in the fairytale world. He worked through his memories and reclaimed them as his own. Eiji's visit to the western castle could not have come at a better time.

He needed to have a little chat with her about the stunt she pulled with the moon robe. It cost him his memories and robbed him of a choice. A choice he should have been allowed to make. He would make her pay for that.

He had sensed her temper flare as soon as she entered the front gates. She was still as reactive as ever. Her lack of control over her emotions nearly made him lose his composure when she saw Ritsuka speaking with him. Eiji's expression had been an instant reminder to be more careful when she was studying his face. He wanted her all to himself when he revealed that he remembered *everything*.

She knows me too well. The thought made the possessive side of his nature content.

For now he could enjoy watching her squirm. Her emotions ran across her face every time she was in his presence. *She wants to know if I remember.*

Sesshoshi knocked on the cedar frame of the shōji screen concealing Eiji's room. He heard the sounds of her shuffling inside before she slid open the door. He stared at her for longer than he should have. Her appearance both delighted and saddened him. Eiji looked lovely, more so than he had ever seen her.

That is not true. She is loveliest laying under you on the forest floor.

Sesshoshi suppressed a smirk.

Her formal kimono and elegant hair style made his breath stop short, but her kimono was made of cheap silk. It looked well worn. The protective part of his wolf yōkai nature wanted to dress her in the finest silks. *She would hate that.* And yet it would please him greatly to try.

Her weapon remained in her room and she held a scroll in her hand. Sesshoshi was about to ask if it was another one of her fairytales. He stopped himself. He had a scribe copy all the fairytales in her possession for Lord Ko, but he did not want to risk speaking of anything too familiar just yet.

"Lord Sesshoshi." Eiji bowed low and when she rose to meet him there was a faint blush on her cheeks. He looked down at his attire. Was that what she was staring at? He wore a dark navy kimono. Usually his haori was white with red embellishments – the colours of the west.

"Follow me." Sesshoshi turned and started walking. He did not look back to see if Eiji followed. He revelled in the feel of her aura, so annoyed at him. The smirk on his face stayed till they arrived at the banquet hall. Sesshoshi moved the shōji screen aside. The decorators had outdone themselves. The room was done up with red and white silks hanging from the trusses. Rare meats and fruits were piled on wooden trays. The smells were pleasing rather than overwhelming, something that was difficult to accomplish at yōkai parties.

Sesshoshi heard Eiji gasp. He glanced down at her enraptured face. He knew he should not linger with her so he gestured to where Lord Ko and the other children played. He did not have to speak for Eiji to understand. She bowed and left him to tend to Lord Ko.

Sesshoshi wandered into the crowds. He needed to stay

focused. This party severed a couple of functions. First, his father had invited humans to the banquet. A first in yōkai-human history. His father needed the humans – the Shogun and several daimyo among them – to feel welcome and not threatened.

Second, the yōkai lords of the north and east, Lord Ryuu and Lord Ide, were merciless to humans. They slaughtered them like cattle if they trespassed on their land. Lord Jou needed the yōkai Lords to meet with the humans and understand that the humans were working on a weapon that could destroy yōkai kind. Lord Jou hoped that this would make the yōkai lords change their practices.

He had felt it. The humans fired it a number of days ago. Sesshoshi theorized it had some foundation in reiki. Eiji's reiki was the most powerful he had come across in years. He hoped she would be able to tell how much power the weapon really held. He wanted her opinion.

When Sesshoshi finally managed to turn his attention away from Eiji, he found his father gathered with Lord Ryuu, Lord Ide, Lord Katakura, the Emperor and the Shogun. *Your talent for bringing people together never ceases to amaze me, father.* Though none of his companions looked happy or even comfortable, Lord Jou spoke easily to those around him, gesturing in a way that made Sesshoshi think he was excited.

"Sesshoshi, my boy, come join me," Lord Jou said. He patted Sesshoshi on the shoulder when he came to stand beside the men.

"We were just telling your father what a gracious host he is," The Emperor said. His wrinkled smile was small and unsteady and yet Sesshoshi felt that he meant his words. *He's afraid.* Sesshoshi flicked his eyes to Lord Ryuu.

"Yes, Lord Jou will associate with anyone," Lord Ryuu said.

Lord Ide laughed. "He's been that way since he was a boy. Look at the pet his son picked up. Lord Ko follows in his father's foot steps."

Sesshoshi narrowed his eyes. He kept him self from

looking at Eiji.

The Shogun met his gaze. "I heard that you, Lord Sesshoshi, were seen around a human village lately." This is exactly the kind of thing his father had wanted. Sesshoshi's visits to Eiji's village would not have gone unnoticed. Little did his father know, he got much more than he bargained for.

"Yes. I retrieve Lord Ko from his time with his... friend," Sesshoshi said.

"You two must bathe often," Lord Ryuu said. His nose crinkled up as if he smelled something unpleasant.

"Only because Lord Ko is filthy from playing in the dirt," Lord Jou said. "He has such fun with his human."

Sesshoshi frowned. *Her name is Eiji.* His yōkai surged at the urge to defend her, but he had to hold his tongue. This conversation was held together by a fraying thread over a flame.

"Better covered in dirt than blood," The Shogun said. "But you wouldn't know much of that would you, Lord Ryuu?"

"I prefer blood." Lord Ryuu shrugged.

"I remember a time when we could visit the hot springs in the north. Your lands have such a large amount of cedar too. It was beautiful," the Emperor said.

"It's nice to have such memories," Lord Ryuu said. His dark blue eyes didn't leave the Emperor's.

"Perhaps we could discuss opening up the boarders again sometime," the Shogun said.

"Never. I do not wish to have humans trouncing through my lands again," Lord Ryuu said.

The Emperor's lip thinned into a line. "There are herbs in the north that we cannot find anywhere else. Herbs that we need to cure certain ailments."

Lord Ryuu picked invisible dirt out of his claws. "That is not my concern."

"People are dying."

"The more the better." Lord Ryuu levelled his gaze on the Emperor.

Hn. Maybe this is that yōkai arrogance Eiji was so

annoyed with.

Lord Jou let out a huffed laugh. "We did not come here tonight to talk of such things. You are here as my guests."

"You're right Lord Jou. How rude of me," the Shogun said. "You know, we've made such a fine weapon. Let us show it to you tomorrow. I believe you will find the demonstration most amusing."

Sesshoshi doubted it. The threat in The Shogun's tone could not be missed. The Shogun wanted to show off his weapon so that Lord Ryuu would know what he would be up against if he continued to slaughter humans on his lands.

"I would be honoured to witness it," Lord Jou said. "Tomorrow morning then, if it pleases you."

"It would," the Shogun said.

"Yes, let us see what this little weapon is the humans have made," Lord Ryuu said. He and Lord Ide chuckled.

Sesshoshi wanted to roll his eyes. He hoped Eiji's night was more entertaining than his.

Lord Katakura was pulled away into another conversation along with the Emperor. Lord Ryuu and Lord Ide disappeared shortly after.

"War is inevitable," Lord Jou said. Sesshoshi glanced at his father.

"How close do you think it is?" Sesshoshi asked.

"Weeks away. The Shogun will demonstrate his weapon. Then Lord Ryuu and Lord Ide will be asked one more time if they will open their boarders. They will have a serious decision to make."

"I can already guess what they will choose."

"Exactly." Lord Jou sighed. Sesshoshi's mother pulled his father away and he was left alone. Sesshoshi sought the quiet of the moment. His eyes started to wander toward Eiji.

Ritsuka pulled up beside him, batting her lashes and all hope for peace was lost.

"Lovely evening is it not?" Ritsuka said.

"Hn." Sesshoshi was not in the mood for this game. The

tension from the previous conversation radiated in his shoulders. His mind was occupied with thoughts of Eiji.

"Would you care to go for a stroll, Lord Sesshoshi? Outside. Alone." Ritsuka's tone was low.

"No." Sesshoshi finally found Eiji in the crowd. She sat at the head of a horde of yōkai children. She held a scroll in her hands. She was reading. Her face shifted expressions as she read. The children surrounding her leaned forward. Some had their mouths hanging open.

"Checking on Lord Ko?" Ritsuka's voice nearly made him jump. He was not distracted long and yet he had forgotten she was there.

"Yes." Sesshoshi was not going to admit the real reason for his inattention.

"How can he stand to be so close to a human?" Ritsuka asked in a way that did not demand an answer. Eiji leaned forward and said something that scared the children. They shrieked, drawing the attention of some of the adults near by. The shrieking turned to laughter. Eiji's smiled was radiant.

"You're watching her." Ritsuka moved to stand in front of him. "Ko's human."

Sesshoshi flicked his gaze down to her. "I observe many."

"Maybe. But I've never seen that look in your eyes before." Ritsuka's frown was deep. "I heard you'd been spending time in a human village."

"I pick up Ko after his time with Eiji."

"Eiji, is it?" Ristuka raised a brow. "How familiar you must be with her to know her name."

Sesshoshi felt no need to defend himself or downplay his interactions with Eiji. The party was slowing down and soon Sesshoshi would be able to claim what was his.

The displeasure of Ritsuka's face was clear.

"Lord Ko does not stop speaking of her," Sesshoshi said. Frustration bubbled off Ristuka's form. She took her leave of him. She must have had enough of his vague answers.

Sesshoshi spent the rest of the party waiting. Waiting for

the party to end. Waiting for the moment where he would confront his priestess.

Chapter 3

Eiji left Lord Ko's room after she tucked him in. A small smile was stuck on her face. The children had loved The Adventures of Kintaro. Lord Ko couldn't stop talking about it as she laid him down to sleep. She knew he would like it.

Her room was easier to find when the halls were nearly empty. Most of the castle's guests were still at the banquet. Eiji tried to hold on to every memory of every bite of food she'd had. She let out a hum of contentment as she remembered the dango.

"Priestess," a voice said behind her. It wasn't Sesshoshi. That was always her first hope. Eiji turned to see Arata stumble toward her. He had had too much sake to drink.

"Good evening, Arata. Enjoying the party?" She continued to walk back to her room. Arata followed her.

"It was fantas- tic," Arata hiccuped. Eiji walked a little faster. His breath reeked and he moved too close. Arata stumbled next to her. He pushed her shoulder and forced her back into the cedar wall behind them.

"I'm going back to my quarters now," Eiji said. "Let me go." She narrowed her eyes.

"You know what would make this party even better?" Arata grinned. Eiji could guess. "A nice lay with a human priestess. All the other samurai would be so jealous." Eiji nearly growled. She was not some play thing for yōkai to have their fun with.

"No, thank you," Eiji said and made to move away from the wall. Arata held her in place. Her anger started to rise and her reiki went with it. She knew it was dangerous to use her reiki in a place with so many yōkai, but surely an exception could be made if she was being threatened.

"I like the way that burns." *Sesshoshi liked it too.* Arata moved closer to her. "Keep going and you'll have half the castle out here. I've heard the whispers. They'd love to be the one to kill you."

"Step back or I'll purify you," Eiji said.

"It would mean your death." Arata laughed.

"And yours." Eiji pushed more of her reiki out, concentrating it where Arata's hands touched her. He hissed and pulled back.

"You whore." Arata lunged for her. Eiji moved to defend herself, but Arata was gone. A thud brought her attention to her left. Sesshoshi had Arata pinned against the floor.

"You are distressing our guests," Sesshoshi growled.

"I'm sorry, my Lord." Arata struggled to breathe. Sesshoshi let him go and Arata scrambled away.

Sesshoshi turned to Eiji. "Your distress was bothering the guests."

Eiji bowed low. "My apologies, my Lord." She shuffled down the hall and put as much distance between herself and Sesshoshi as she could. She hated the way he looked at her now. Like she was nothing to him. *Because you are. And it's all your fault.*

Eiji sunk onto her futon when she reached her room. She shrugged her kimono off. Eiji removed the pins decorating her hair and let it tumble free. It had been a long night. Eiji fell asleep as soon as she closed her eyes.

In the middle of the night a yōkai aura woke her. Yōkai auras surrounded her in this place, but this one was right on top of her.

Eiji's eye shot open and she sat up.

There was a girl crouched at the edge of her futon. Eiji recognized her as the yōkai that had hovered close to Sesshoshi during the banquet. Eiji didn't like the look in her eyes.

"So you are the one my Lord Sesshoshi had his eyes on tonight," she said.

"Sorry, my Lady. What is your name?" Eiji said, bowing low. She was so tired but she needed to remain as polite as possible.

"I'm Ritsuka of the red panda clan," she said. "I hope to be Lord Sesshoshi's future mate." Eiji pushed down her jealousy. It wouldn't be wise to lose her temper with Ritsuka. Eiji could tell.

"I see," Eiji said. "It's an honour to meet you."

Ritsuka growled. "Don't play polite with me girl. I'm here to tell you to stay away from Lord Sesshoshi. You are human." Ritsuka said it as if Eiji's race explained something obvious.

"If I'm human and of no interest to Lord Sesshoshi then why are you here?"

"You bitch," Ritsuka growled. She made to lunge for Eiji but Eiji brought out her reiki. Her palms glowed pink. Ritsuka stopped. She seemed to be thinking about her next move. *She doesn't want to draw attention to her being here. Lucky for me.*

"I don't want to fight with you. You may dote on Lord Sesshoshi all you like. I won't stand in your way, but please do not threaten me when I'm a guest in his home," Eiji said.

Ritsuka backed down. "He is mine."

"Of course," Eiji agreed, trying not to roll her eyes. Ritsuka seemed happy with her answer and rose. She slipped silently out through the shōji screen and left Eiji alone.

Eiji flopped back down onto her bed. For all of Sesshoshi's boasts of yōkai superiority and their self control, Eiji had sure had an emotion filled night. She longed for home. She wanted to be back where she didn't have to be around Sesshoshi, or any yōkai for that matter. She didn't think she could take much more yōkai attention tonight.

24

Chapter 4

Sesshoshi lay awake.

It was the hour of the tiger and the castle was quiet. Sesshoshi rose and headed for the guest quarters. Almost everyone was sleeping including the guards. Usually he would reprimand them, but the rules were loose on banquet nights.

He slipped into Eiji's room when he found her door.

Sesshoshi watched her sleep for a few moments. He took in her beauty without interruption for the first time since she arrived.

He flared his aura and Eiji shot up.

"Leave me alone Lady Ritsuka. I just want to sleep," Eiji mumbled. Sesshoshi sniffed the air. Ritsuka had been here. He was too distracted by Eiji to notice Ritsuka's faded scent in the room.

Eiji looked up and saw him. Her eyes widened and her mouth dropped open. Sesshoshi smirked. He could not help but stare at her lips.

"Sesshoshi," Eiji said. She met his gaze and held it for what seemed an eternity. She shook her head several time. "Oh, no. No, no, no."

"No, little priestess?" He knelt down on the edge of her futon and crawled toward her. Eiji backed away from him, but not in earnest. In two strides he was in front of her, their noses only inches apart.

"You remember," Eiji said. He was pleased she could read him so easily.

"I do," Sesshoshi said. "We need to talk. You and I. About the moon robe." He growled and enjoyed the way she shivered.

"The - The moon robe. I, uh -" Eiji floundered. Sesshoshi would hear her explanation later. It had been too long since he had touched her. He grabbed her arm and pulled her against his body. He captured her lips and revelled in the way Eiji collapsed against him. He knew she built up walls to protect herself from her feelings for him. That was why she had used the moon robe. But now that they were together again, the way her body responded to his meant she could no longer lie to him.

Sesshoshi slid his arm around her waist and pushed on the small of her back to bring her closer. Eiji tangled her fingers in his hair. He thoroughly enjoyed it when she did. All his nerve endings tingled one by one. She ran her slim fingers along the shell of his pointed ear. She threaded them through his hair and along the back of his neck. Sesshoshi deepened the kiss, running his tongue along her bottom lip. Eiji's moans were music to his ears. He had waited a long time to hear them, to taste her again, to touch her. He moved his hands to the inside of her cotton kimono. Her skin was smooth and warm.

Eiji broke their kiss and pulled back. Sesshoshi stopped moving.

"Sesshoshi. We can't. Not here in the castle. I haven't even said hello to you properly," Eiji said.

He chuckled. "That is true. The hello part, not the part about the castle. This is my home. I can do what I wish."

Eiji rested her forehead against his. "I can't. Everyone will know. They'll, well, they might kill me." They would already know. Sesshoshi could smell his scent on her already. Everyone in the western castle would know they were close by tomorrow morning.

"No one will touch what is mine," Sesshoshi said. He lay on the futon and pulled her down next to him. He ran his claws along her arm. Eiji sighed.

"Why was Ritsuka in your room?" Sesshoshi asked.

Eiji let out a rueful laugh. "She came to tell me that you are hers and that I should stay away from you." He growled, which made Eiji giggle. "I wasn't going to listen to her. Unless you had lost your memories for good."

"Yes. About that," Sesshoshi began.

"Look, I'm sorry. I was scared you would reject me when

we got back home. And if you did want to be with me, then I didn't want to make you choose between your family and me," Eiji said.

"What makes you think I will have to choose?" Sesshoshi chuckled. "I can do as I please."

"Your parents won't be happy."

"Perhaps. But you did not know that for certain. I think they will like you just fine." Sesshoshi touched the side of her face, running his thumb over her cheek. "We will find out tomorrow I suppose." Eiji shot up, propped up on her elbow, looking down at him.

"Tomorrow? No, you have to leave my room before anyone knows you're here. I can't bring this upon you," Eiji said. Tears were starting to form in the corners of her eyes. Sesshoshi could not understand what upset her so.

"*You* are not bringing anything upon me," Sesshoshi said. He rose up to kiss her, pulling her down on top of him. "I am a big boy. I can confront the consequences of my actions."

Eiji sighed. "Now's not the time for jokes." Her dark eyes looked into his.

"But they are so rare coming from me, I thought you would at least smile." Sesshoshi grinned and kissed her again. Eiji relaxed in his hold. He moved her to lay beside him once again. "Now where were we?"

"Sesshoshi!" Eiji's final protest was weak. As soon as his hands found her breast she could not breathe. His hands roamed her entire body, pulling her yukata away as he went. He found the spot between her legs that made her arch her back against the futon. He worked it until she was a shuddering mess beneath him. Once she found her release, Sesshoshi slid on top of her and then in.

"How could you make me forget this," Sesshoshi said as he moved inside her. "But you were allowed to remember."

"Would you believe it was as torturous for me as it was for you?"

"No."

Eiji laughed and Sesshoshi felt her warm breath against his ear. It did not take long before both of them were spent. He pulled out of her and it sent one last shiver down his spine. Sesshoshi lay back on the futon and Eiji curled into his side.

Eiji let out a deep sigh. "The banquet was... tense."

Sesshoshi chuckled. "So you noticed?"

"How could I not. What happened?"

"Lord Ryuu bragged about killing humans. And now the Shogun wants to gift my father a demonstration of his weapon. Which will also show Lord Ryuu what he is in for if he continues to slaughter humans that enter the northern lands."

"He'll have to learn to share."

"Perhaps."

"They were our lands. A long time ago, at least."

"No they were not."

Eiji gave him a look. One that said 'yeah, sure, yōkai.' "What will we do about the weapon? What if it really is as powerful as the Shogun says?"

"We will have to wait until morning to find out." Sesshoshi held her close. There was no doubt in his mind about his course of action. Eiji slept eventually and then Sesshoshi closed his eyes to the darkness.

Sesshoshi slept well for the first time since he had recovered memories of Eiji wrapped in his arms. He took a deep breath and exhaled with a rumble. Eiji snuggled closer. Sesshoshi felt the change in her breathing. She was close to waking.

He brushed her hair away from her face just as Eiji's eyes fluttered open.

"Good morning."

Eiji's eyes grew wide. Sesshoshi heard her heart race. He watched emotions scrawl over her face.

"Sesshoshi... you stayed the night," Eiji said.

"Did I give any indication that I would not?"

"No. I just..."

"You can stop thinking all the things you are already

thinking. I would say humans have an amazing ability to second guess everything they do. But I believe that pertains only to you." Sesshoshi smirked at Eiji's annoyed look. "Let us have some breakfast."

Once they dressed, Sesshoshi led Eiji, hair bound and scythe chained at her side, through the halls of the western palace. Eiji's unease radiated off her in waves. She smelled like him and Sesshoshi revelled in it. Any yōkai would know Eiji was his from miles away.

Usually members of the western palace were wise enough to avert their gaze when Sesshoshi neared. Their reactions this morning were delayed. Everyone they passed stared as long as they dared.

Eiji held Sesshoshi's arm as she walked next to him. Sesshoshi spotted Ritsuka up ahead. She gawked openly, her mouth hung slack. She looked like a fish. *How amusing.* Sesshoshi smirked.

"Good morning Lord Sesshoshi," Ritsuka bowed.

"Good morning," Sesshoshi replied. He placed a hand on the small of Eiji's back and guided her around the stunned yōkai.

Sesshoshi bent down to whisper in Eiji's ear. "Stay here a moment." When she nodded he felt the faint movement against his cheek.

Sesshoshi turned and strode back to Ritsuka. He cleared his throat and she nearly jumped out of her skin. Ritsuka looked up at him with wide eyes. "Yes, my Lord?"

"It would be wise if you stayed away from what is mine," Sesshoshi said. Ritsuka's mouth twisted in a way that made him wonder if she would dispute him. Her ire pushed against his yōkai.

Ritsuka's lips set into a fake smile. "Of course, my Lord."

"Good." Sesshoshi returned to Eiji's side and led her the rest of the way to the dining hall. Lord Ko and his parents were already there. Lord Ko's eyes brightened at the sight of Eiji. He left his seat and sped toward her.

"Lord Ko. Sit down. A young Lord does not leave the

table in the middle of a meal," Satori said. His mother kept her eyes on Eiji.

"Sorry mother," Ko said. He sped back to his seat.

Eiji knelt next to Sesshoshi and bowed. She placed her hands together on the floor and touched her forehead to the back of her hands. "I'm honoured to be in your presence."

"You may rise, child," Jou said. His father looked amused by Eiji's formality, but Sesshoshi knew some Lords would kill for anything less than a show of the highest respect. "Sit."

Eiji took a seat on a cushion around the table.

The silence in the room felt heavy on Sesshoshi's shoulders.

"Eiji, will you play with me today?" Ko asked. Ko was not oblivious to the tension in the room. He likely did not understand what it meant and did not care for the formality of adults.

"Today we must watch the Shogun display his weapon for us," Eiji said, displeasure thick in her tone. "If you'll allow me, I'll sit with you my Lord."

Ko's eyes brightened. "Yes!"

"Sit among us?" Satori tilted her head. "As if you are part of *our* family?"

Eiji's face grew red. "I'm sorry. I meant no disrespect. I forgot my place."

"As my intended you are more than welcome," Sesshoshi said.

His mother growled.

His father choked on his breakfast. "Your intended?"

"Yay!" Lord Ko clapped his hands.

"Did I miss something? When exactly did you make Lord Ko's human your intended?"

"Intended?" Eiji's quiet, questioning voice drew his attention to her.

"Like a fiancé."

"Hey! When did we decide that? Don't make decisions for me," Eiji hissed. Sesshoshi could tell she was trying to be quiet, as if to keep the conversation between just the two of them. A hopeless goal when surrounded by yōkai.

"You are one to talk, little priestess."

"That was different."

"I fail to see how."

"It was and you know it."

"I do not."

Eiji glared at him and Sesshoshi stared back. He felt his father's mood shift. Something in the conversation between Eiji and him had pleased his father.

"Very well. Welcome to the clan Eiji," Lord Jou said.

Eiji's wide brown eyes looked to Sesshoshi for clarification. He could give her none. He only gave her a small smile and turned back to his breakfast.

"So, you can sit with me?" Lord Ko said.

"Yes."

"Yay!"

Sesshoshi took a bite of the fish on his plate. *To be a child again. Life is viewed through clear eyes that see nothing.*

The rest of their meal passed in silence. Eiji followed Sesshoshi out to the courtyard once they were dismissed. Sesshoshi followed her gaze as she looked up. Eiji's stare was fixated on the statue of one of his ancient relatives.

"Do all yōkai have a... beast form like that?" Eiji asked.

"I thought you would know," Sesshoshi said.

She looked at him. "I always thought lesser yōkai were beasts, but higher yōkai look like humans... with a few modifications." Her gaze travelled to Sesshoshi's pointed ears.

"That is mostly true. Lesser yōkai are always in their beast form. That is what makes them so unpleasant. But all yōkai have a beast form. Even the higher ones,"

"Even you?"

"Even me."

"Can I see it?" Eiji's body buzzed with excitement. It pleased him greatly. And yet...

"No." Sesshoshi did not enjoy watching Eiji's face fall. She looked dejected. "It is not that I do not wish to show you.

Yōkai must be careful with when and how long they channel their beast. It is the most primal part of us and it wants to take over. I have watched yōkai in my own family go crazy from too much time spent in their beast form. I cannot call it forth just to show you." Eiji's shoulders relaxed as she let out a sigh. She sounded like Ko when no one would play with him.

"Fine. I understand," Eiji said.

"Maybe you will see it one day."

She smiled. "Maybe?"

"Maybe. Though I hope not."

Sesshoshi led Eiji to the back part of the western castle. The open balcony on their left overlooked the forest surrounding the castle. Other yōkai were gathered there already. They parted and made way for him. Many of them took a second glance at Eiji, but no one dared comment.

Sesshoshi took his place beside his father. Ko ran into Eiji's arms. She picked him up and held him so he could see over the cedar railing.

Lord Ryuu stood beside his father. "You allow these humans too much liberty, Lord Jou." Lord Ryuu fixed a scathing glare on Eiji's back. Sesshoshi growled low. Lord Ryuu would hear it and if he was wise he would not mention Eiji in this discussion.

"Times are changing Lord Ryuu. I choose to adapt while you choose to fight. I only hope we will both have good outcomes," Lord Jou said.

"I will know my fortunes once the humans display this weapon of theirs. It will be nothing more than a match stick," Lord Ryuu said.

"I hope you are right," Lord Jou said.

Down below the human samurai hauled a lesser yōkai toward a post. The beast struggled but the men overpowered it. They tied the creature to the post and ran back to the weapon.

The weapon resembled the canons that came from the barbarians that sailed in from the north. Sesshoshi had seen one before, but had not taken interest in it. The canon alone would not be enough to kill a higher yōkai.

Sesshoshi was tempted to scoff at the Shogun and his subjects. Did he really think yōkai would fear a canon? But Sesshoshi was not a fool. He knew the humans were not stupid. This weapon looked like a canon but he was sure it would not behave like one.

The Shogun joined them on the balcony. "Thank you for coming. We hope you will like this demonstration. The advances we have made thanks to the travellers from the north makes this our finest weapon." The Shogun inclined his head and the samurai below prepared the weapon.

There was a feeling in the air. *Like when Eiji's powers surface.* It came from the weapon.

All yōkai recoiled as the weapon's power grew. Pink light shone in the barrel of the canon.

Eiji sucked in a breath. Sesshoshi could see her grip tightening around Ko.

The canon fired a blast of energy at the lesser yōkai. It melted like ice on a hot day. The blast contained more power than it needed to kill the yōkai. Sesshoshi knew that much power could have killed a yōkai of his calibre. That was the point of the demonstration. Every yōkai around him knew it.

Lord Ryuu spat at the Shogun's feet, but the man ignored it. In fact, he looked almost pleased to have gotten such a reaction out of Lord Ryuu. Lord Jou remained silent. His jaw was tight. The energy from the canon slowly dissipated.

The Shogun clapped his hands together. "What a show! Impressive isn't it?"

Sesshoshi's mouth twisted. The Shogun continued to act as if this demonstration had been for entertainment instead of what it really was.

A message.

Look at the weapon we have made. If you cross us we will destroy you.

Chapter 5

Eiji felt sick, like when she was child and would eat too many sweets at Obon. The power pulsing from the canon licked against her skin in a way that made it feel too tight. The lesser yōkai and the pole it'd been tied to was gone.

Eiji held Lord Ko tighter.

Eiji listened to the Shogun praise the weapon. She could never say anything that went against him, but Eiji wanted to give him a piece of her mind. *This is barbaric!* And it was, but yōkai had been even less kind to humans for centuries before this moment. Humans never had a way to fight back before. A weapon like the Shogun's meant humans could finally rise in the ranks. They would be seen as a threat by yōkai, not just something in their way. Yōkai like Lord Ryuu could no longer exterminate humans living on his lands and lesser yōkai couldn't rampage whenever they felt like it.

But we can't be just like them. Eiji felt it in the core of her being. *All this fighting will never get us anywhere.*

Eiji's senses shifted through the bits of the canon's power that still hung in the air. There was definitely reiki in the mix, but it wasn't very stable. *I wish I could ask grandmother about this.*

Lord Jou cleared his throat. "Yes, well, that was quite the demonstration. Very impressive indeed. You and your subjects must be ready for tea. Let us retire and I will happily host you." Lady Satori took Lord Ko from Eiji's arms and followed her mate down the hall. Eiji watched them go. Lord Jou spoke like he would to old friends about to settle down for some sake. Lady Satori's lips were pulled in a thin line while she held her son as protectively as Eiji had moments ago.

"Thank you Lord Jou," the Shogun said. Lord Jou led them away, leaving Eiji and Sesshoshi alone with the other yōkai lords.

Once the others were out of earshot, Lord Ryuu growled. "Those humans seek to destroy our kind."

"That's a little dramatic, Lord Ryuu," Lord Katakura said. His tone was that of someone speaking to a child.

"That kind of thinking will be your downfall," Lord Ryuu said. "Lord Jou appears to want to play along with the humans as well."

"My father aims to preserve our kind and improve relations with humans," Sesshoshi said.

"You seem to be doing your part, pup," Lord Ryuu nearly spat at Sesshoshi's feet. Eiji frowned and clenched her fists. Her reiki flared.

"Feisty isn't she," Lord Ryuu laughed in a way that wasn't kind. "A priestess. You will be the death of each other. Yōkai and humans are not meant to be *together.*"

Sesshoshi was silent but there was a dangerous glint to his gaze. Lord Ryuu seemed to find that amusing. He laughed to himself and left them with a look of disdain. The other Lords followed, some going after Lord Ryuu while others made a path for Lord Jou.

When Eiji and Sesshoshi were left alone she turned to him. "I've never felt anything so powerful."

"I have," Sesshoshi said.

Eiji's brows scrunched together. "When?"

"You. You have just as much reiki as that machine. Probably more."

"I do not," Eiji said.

"You do. You cannot feel it, but I can."

Eiji sighed. "Maybe I do, but what does it matter? Even if I could destroy the weapon, the humans will make more." Sesshoshi smirked at her and Eiji rolled her eyes. *I'm human too.* "*We* will make more."

"Perhaps," Sesshoshi said. "Humans and yōkai will continue to kill each other long after both of us are gone. I only care that it is a fair fight."

"I agree and yet it hasn't been a fair fight since it started."

Eiji looked up to meet Sesshoshi's gaze. This was one of the reasons she used the moon robe on him. This tension that came from the differences in their life experiences.

Sesshoshi tilted his head and his expression said *this again?*

"What? You know it's true," Eiji said.

"Hn," Sesshoshi nodded. "I suppose it is. And yet you agree that the weapon must have a match?"

"Yes. I was thinking the same thing. Humans can't become what yōkai have always been. We're not made for that. The Shogun likely thinks he's found a way to dominate all of Japan. That's a dangerous desire."

Sesshoshi's small smile made Eiji's stomach flutter. He was pleased with her.

"By the end of the day my father will have a better idea of where we stand with the Shogun," Sesshoshi said. "We can decide what to do later."

Later. How much time will we have before the Shogun uses the weapon everyday?

Sesshoshi tapped Eiji's forehead with his clawed finger. "I can hear you thinking."

Eiji smiled a little. "I just- I don't like not knowing how much time we have before this becomes a problem. A big problem."

"Do you think we could destroy the weapon?"

"Maybe. Hm. If I could use reiki it would have to be manipulated somehow. The blast felt different from my power. More like reiki woven together. Fragile and unstable. I couldn't just blast the weapon with my reiki, but my grandmother knew about these-" Eiji searched for the right word. "manipulations. A way to undo reiki held together like that. I wish I could ask her about them."

Sesshoshi worked his jaw. He was hiding something from her.

"What?"

Sesshoshi sighed. "I may know a way you could speak

with your grandmother."

Eiji stumbled on her feet. She felt like a worm yōkai had hit her in the stomach. "You what?"

"I believe we can speak with her."

"You have some explaining to do."

"In the fairytale world, when the unfinished song took you, a woman appeared in a doorway. She invited me inside and it was not hard to recognize this woman as your grandmother. Her name was Tsuru. Perhaps she would have the same knowledge as your real grandmother had," Sesshoshi said. His golden eyes studied her as he waited for her to speak.

"My real grandmother? Sesshoshi, she *is* my real grandmother. How could you hide this from me?" Tears burned at the corner of Eiji's eyes.

"She is not your real grandmother. Your real grandmother is dead. Tsuru told me not to speak a word of our meeting to you because she was worried you would make this very mistake." Sesshoshi wiped away her tears with the back of his hand. "She worried you would think she was real and refuse to leave the fairytale world. I did not disagree with her."

"That wasn't your choice to make," Eiji sobbed. Her chest hurt. Her grandmother had been there, in the fairytale world, and she'd been so close to seeing her once again.

"Do not speak to me about choices, little priestess." Sesshoshi's tone was dangerous. "Now you know what it feels like to have the choice to stay with a loved one taken from you. I kept Tsuru a secret because I was asked by a woman that was very concerned for your well being, not to hurt you."

Eiji tried to process what he was telling her but all her mind could focus on was *"loved one."* Her mouth went dry. She pushed her feelings down.

"I want to see her. I have to. And now I have a question for her," Eiji said.

"Of course," Sesshoshi said. "Let us return to your village. We can enter the fairytale world once again to look for her."

Eiji nodded. *Grandma, I get to see you again. I miss you*

so much.

Down below, Eiji watched the samurai pack up the canon. The Shogun was with them now and it appeared he and the Emperor were leaving.

"Let us find my father."

Eiji nodded and followed Sesshoshi down the halls. They found Lord Jou in the courtyard.

"Father, how did it go with the Shogun?"

Lord Jou shook his head. "Lord Ryuu came in and disrupted our tea. He and the Shogun got into an argument and declared war on one another. We have only a few days before they will begin fighting."

"What is our role?" Sesshoshi asked.

"The west will aid the Shogun if he needs it, but I tried to tell him that and he said he needs only his weapon. I will not help someone who does not wish it."

"A few days." Sesshoshi frowned.

That doesn't give us much time. Eiji bit her bottom lip.

Sesshoshi informed his family he would take Eiji home and that he would return shortly. Lord Ko hugged her good-bye. Eiji bowed to the Lord and Lady of the west before following Sesshoshi through the castle and out the front gates.

"We do not have much time. We must learn as much as we can about destroying the weapon before the Shogun or Lord Ryuu can do anything drastic," Sesshoshi said.

"We should travel quickly. Like in your beast form," Eiji said, trying to sound casual.

Sesshoshi let out a low chuckle, the kind that did *things* to her. "No. But nice try, little priestess." He knelt down in front of her and, with what felt like the entire western castle watching them, Eiji climbed onto Sesshoshi's back. He hooked his arms under her legs and once Eiji's arms were secure around his neck he took off.

Eiji squeaked. She'd forgotten how it felt to travel at yōkai speed. The dusty path leading out of the western palace was busy. Humans and yōkai stared as they passed. Eiji doubted they could tell who was riding on Sesshoshi's back, but the sight was odd enough that it called for open gaping.

"How much time do you think we have?" Eiji said against the shell of Sesshoshi's ear.

He shifted underneath her. "I do not know, but if I remember correctly time moves slower inside the fairytale world."

"How do you know? You couldn't remember we had been in the fairytale world."

"Hmm, yes. I could not remember because *you* placed the moon robe on my shoulders and took my memories."

"Sesshoshi," Eiji said in a tone that was meant to warn him not to test her, but was received with little more than a chuckle.

"I believe no more than an hour passed."

"We were gone for *days.*"

"Yes, but the scribe from the castle had only just arrived when I left you in the hut," Sesshoshi said.

Eiji nodded against his shoulder. "That means we should have several days to find my grandmother and see if we can destroy the weapon."

Eiji's body lurched as Sesshoshi came to a sudden stop. She yelped as he swung her down off his back and onto her feet. Eiji had just found her footing when Sesshoshi pulled her forward. He leaned down and captured her lips in a firm kiss. Eiji melted against him, curving her body into his.

She heard other travellers around her gasp. There were whispers of "Is that Lord Sesshoshi? Is he kissing a... human?"

Eiji's cheeks grew warm.

He pulled away from her. "We will have time." Sesshoshi kissed her forehead. Eiji nodded. She climbed back on his back and he took off once again.

It took them much less time to reach Eiji's village than it had for Eiji to reach the western castle. She returned home with a sense of nostalgia even though she hadn't been gone long. Much had changed. It made her home feel too small for her problems.

Sesshoshi put her down at the edge of town.

"Where is the cursed scroll?" Sesshoshi asked.

"In my home," Eiji replied. She led him to her small hut. It looked meagre and plain compared to the western castle. Before she could enter her home, Haruka appeared in front of her. Her eyes flicked to Sesshoshi and then back to Eiji. Eiji knew Haruka should bow to him. Haruka likely knew it too, but Haruka was Haruka and she only focused on one thing at a time.

Haruka's lips thinned. "Explain."

"Explain what?" Eiji blinked.

"*Explain what? Explain* that!" Haruka pointed at Sesshoshi.

"It's Lord Sesshoshi," Eiji said. Her face grew warm.

"I know – gah! Look, when you went to sort out your grandmother's things, you came back smelling like Lord Sesshoshi. I didn't ask you about it because you didn't seem too interested in talking. And then a few months passed and I never saw him near the village again. But now you disappear off to the western castle and you've returned with him. You smell of him, *again.*" Haruka's eyes started to tear. "I thought we were best friends. But best friends don't hide things like *this* from one another. I'm so dishonoured. Perhaps I should just end my life to avoid further disgrace."

Eiji sighed. *So dramatic, Haruka.* She glanced back at Sesshoshi. The amusement in his eyes made her relax. "Haruka, I wanted to tell you, I just-"

Sesshoshi leaned over her shoulder. She could feel the warmth of his cheek next to hers. "I've been keeping her busy."

You're no better than her, Sesshoshi.

Haruka's eyes went wide. She looked like she was struggling to find her words. "Yup. Of course, my Lord. Right."

Sesshoshi leaned away from her and Eiji placed a hand on Haruka's forearm. The half-breed nearly jumped out of her skin. Haruka refocused her gaze on Eiji. "We'll talk. I promise."

"Fine." Haruka narrowed her eyes. Eiji knew she wasn't really mad, not deep down. "We'll talk later." Haruka was gone as quick as she'd come.

"Your friend is very strange," Sesshoshi chuckled.

"You can say that again," Eiji muttered as she pushed open the shōji screen and went inside. "Father. I've returned." Eiji found her home empty.

"I can sense your father a little ways to the east."

"He must be working," Eiji said. She felt a pang of guilt that she wasn't out there helping him.

"Let us go to the fairytale world before he returns. It will be easier if we do not have to explain it to him. We can see him after."

Eiji nodded. "Let's go." She went to her room and dug the scroll out of its hiding place, a box hidden under a pile of fairytales.

She interlaced her fingers with Sesshoshi's and touched the scroll.

44

Chapter 6

They were back inside the peach pit. Sesshoshi remembered it well. Eiji had become so annoyed with him back then. She was irritated by all his comments about his superior senses. He smirked. He had enjoyed stirring her emotions since the day he met her. Her lack of respect for him had bothered him at first. He had not had much regard for her. Though he found her interesting and amusing. It had not taken long before Eiji had bewitched him completely and he was happy to surrender to her.

Eiji stood close this time. She moved even closer as their confines started to bob and sway. The peach pit moved down river just as before. Eiji lost her footing and Sesshoshi snaked his arm around her waist, pulling her to him to steady her.

"I missed you." Eiji's voice was quiet in the darkness, but he heard her clearly. He sensed she wanted to say more. Sesshoshi tightened his hold on her.

"I missed you a lot," Eiji said. "You've discovered how I can be. I thought using the moon robe would solve everything. You would forget me. I would move on. Neither of us would have to deal with the consequences of our... relationship. But everyday I woke up feeling alone. I was empty and hollow without you. Haruka could see it. My father too, but we didn't speak of it. I was wrong. I couldn't move on. Now that you're by my side again I can't-" Eiji's voice cut off. She was crying.

Sesshoshi ran his hands through her hair. A rumble came from deep in his chest. It was something wolf yōkai did to calm distressed loved ones. "It was foolish of you to think you could hide from me."

"I always think I can do things on my own." Eiji wiped her tears with the back of her sleeve. "That I can be happy alone. I've told myself that for so long because I don't want to leave my father alone. He already lost my mother. I don't want him to lose me."

"That is noble of you, but not sustainable. Does your own happiness matter so little?"

"Haruka says the same thing, just less elegantly."

Sesshoshi chuckled. He leaned down and kissed Eiji's lips. They tasted salty from her tears. Sesshoshi ran his tongue along her bottom lip and Eiji pushed herself closer to him. His hands brushed over the curve of her ribs, over the fabric of her hakui. Eiji's hand found their way into his hair and along his scalp. Sesshoshi growled under her touch.

Sesshoshi sighed against her lips and pulled back. "The old childless couple are about to cut us out."

Eiji laughed and sniffled away the last of her tears. "I wonder who will be Momotaro this time." Sunlight shone through the top of the peach pit. Sesshoshi jumped out with Eiji in his grasp. Granny and Grandpa towered above them, just as before. *This world really is so cyclical. Everything is the same.*

"Oh my! A little boy!" Granny said.

"A little boy inside the peach! How marv-"

"I'm going to stop you right there," Eiji said just as they started to grow to their regular size. The elderly couple stopped talking. That meant they could hear her.

"You're Momotaro again," Sesshoshi said.

"It must be because I'm braver and stronger than you. And my acting skills are superior."

"Hn. If you say so, little priestess."

"We have visitors again, don't we?" Granny said.

"Yes. Same ones as before," Eiji said. "Do you remember us?"

"The girl and the yōkai lord?" Grandpa said. Eiji nodded. His face scrunched up. "The monkey told us about how you slaughtered the oni. Many, many times."

Eiji looked at her feet and kicked at the sand. "Right. Well, we're back."

It bothers her that they are not pleased to see her. Sesshoshi smirked. He would never understand it: Eiji's desire to be liked by everyone she meets. Even so, it was a trait he would like her to keep.

"We need to find my grandmother. She wrote herself into the Overworld," Eiji said.

Granny nodded slowly. "O-Ok. Do you know where to look? She could be anywhere."

"No, not yet." Eiji glanced at Sesshoshi. "Did she say how we could find her again when you spoke to her?"

"No," Sesshoshi said. "She just appeared after you were taken by the unfinished project. She seemed to reside in her own realm."

"I'm hoping she'll appear to us in the Overworld if we just go there," Eiji said.

"That is rather optimistic," Sesshoshi said.

Granny's smile tightened. "It would be dangerous to stay in the Overworld for long. Travelling between stories is dodgy enough. If you don't know where you're going it would mean giving the unfinished works more time to find you."

"I know all about that." Eiji shuddered.

"We don't know much about the Overworld. We couldn't tell you exactly how to find her," Grandpa said.

"Momotaro! You are so strong and so brave. There are oni causing trouble on Onigashima. Will you not do something?"

Sesshoshi turned to see the peasant from last time running toward them.

Eiji grinned. "Of course I will. I'll go fight them and return with great treasure!"

"Eiji," Sesshoshi growled.

"Oh come on, you're no fun." Eiji rolled her eyes. She turned to the man. "I'll slay the oni."

"Thank you Momotaro," the man said.

Granny pulled a sack loose from a twine belt around her plump waist. "Here child, take these dumplings with you." She placed the bag in Eiji's hands. "Please think carefully about spending time in the Overworld."

"We will."

Sesshoshi and Eiji headed down the path leading to Onigashima. Eiji looked up at him. He could sense he was about to be annoyed by what she was going to say.

"You know, even though we have more time in the fairytale world, we shouldn't waste it," Eiji began. "I know just the thing that will get us to Onigashima faster."

Sesshoshi knew. "What?"

"Your true yōkai form!"

"No. We can walk or you can hop on my back again," Sesshoshi said. There was part of him that was pleased Eiji did not shy away from his yōkai nature, but the yōkai beast inside him would try to tear him apart. Yōkai are calamity itself. Sesshoshi's human-like form kept his yōkai sealed while allowing him filtered access to its power. It was best to keep the beast chained.

Eiji pouted. Sesshoshi ignored her.

They soon encountered the dog. Eiji was quick to explain that she and her yōkai lord had returned. The dog paled. "I'm going to run ahead and warn the others."

"Oh. Alright." Eiji frowned. "Wait, dog." The dog stopped mid-step. "How long has it been since we were last here?"

"Oh, I don't know, a dozen thousand cycles or so," the dog said. He took off running near the end of his sentence.

"Well, that told me almost nothing," Eiji said.

"It is irrelevant. Time does not work the same here as it does at home."

They found Onigashima easily and the animals waited for them on the shore. Eiji gave them all a dumpling. It might be necessary to advance the story, but Eiji likely did it because she wanted the animals to like her again.

"I will return." Sesshoshi left Eiji on the beach. He leapt onto the boat resting on the shore. The first time he had helped Eiji into the boat. The curve of her body against his had sparked something within him, something that he could no longer ignore.

The boat ran ashore on Onigashima. Sesshoshi strolled onto the white sand. The oni would not see him coming.

His yōkai rushed through his fingers. Sesshoshi's yōkai blades shot from his finger tips when he swiped his claws at the oni. They fell to pieces. The first time around they had waited for the pheasant to sneak in and unlock the door for them, but this time Sesshoshi waited for no one.

He moved through the oni like a storm. *I do not see why the animals find this so repulsive. There is honour in death.* Sesshoshi did not waste time or toy with his victims. They died quickly and neatly. Once finished, Sesshoshi packed up the treasure and returned to shore.

"Here," Sesshoshi said. Eiji told the animals to take the treasure back to Momotaro's parents. They did so without another word.

"This time around was better, less talking and theatrics," Sesshoshi said.

Eiji huffed. "So boring."

Sesshoshi saw the white oval light at the far end of the beach. It would take them to the Overworld.

"Once we are in the Overworld do you think she'll come to us?" Eiji asked. For a moment Sesshoshi did not know if Eiji spoke of her grandmother or the unfinished project that grabbed her last time. "We will find your grandmother. Last time she found me. She will come for you," Sesshoshi said.

"We were in the Overworld many times during our last visit. She didn't come for me," Eiji said. "Just you."

"She was afraid you would not leave. I told her that she had recently died in our world and that convinced her even more," Sesshoshi said. "She was right to worry. Your attachment is so strong, you risk not letting go of a ghost."

"She's not a ghost!" Eiji yelled, turning on him.

Sesshoshi placed a hand on her shoulder. Eiji's posture softened. "She is not a ghost, no. But she is not your real grandmother either."

"I know."

"I hope you do."

"Sesshoshi... Forget it." Eiji's anger rose again. She

stomped toward the white oval light and jumped into the
Overworld a couple steps ahead of him. Hot panic ran through his
veins at the thought of losing her to an unfinished project a
second time. Sesshoshi was through the portal in a flash.

He found Eiji safe on the other side.

"Grandmother!" Eiji shouted. "Grandmother!" Eiji
wandered through the Overworld calling for Tsuru. Sesshoshi
kept his eyes open for unfinished works. He saw them all around.
The creatures began to take notice of them. The unfinished moved
closer.

Sesshoshi could destroy them with his claws and move
Eiji away from them when needed, but he worried he would not
be able to hold them off forever.

"Eiji, how did you defeat the unfinished song that grabbed
you?"

"I made new verses."

"What were they?"

Eiji stopped walking. She seemed to look around for the
first time. The unfinished works surrounded them and yet none
were too close, yet.

Then Eiji began to sing in a soft voice.

Eiji, Eiji
Girl in a dream
Crying at the corner of town
In twilight after dawn
Near the edge of the moon
Who'll defend you now?

Sesshoshi, Sesshoshi
Wolf in a cave
Backed by honour and doubt
Caught in the middle
Of a great divide
Who'll find you out?

Eiji, Eiji.
Not what it seems
Love, affection and drought.
In the dragon's tear
The weak of heart reside
Who's your leader now?

Chapter 7

Sesshoshi stared at her after she finished her song. "Somehow I feel I understand you better."

"Oh."

"Eiji, we must leave the Overworld. I cannot hold them off forever. I had thought whatever you had done to defeat that song before might have had some effect on any unfinished being. It appears I was wrong."

Eiji's shoulders drooped. "And I was so sure my grandmother would appear to me when we came here."

"It was a valid theory, but it is not working. We must retreat to a fairytale," Sesshoshi said. He was right. *Grandma might be hiding in one of the fairytales. But which one? She would hide in her favourite story, but she's said all of them were her favourite at one point.*

Then Eiji remembered the scroll. The one inside The Snow Woman. "I think she's in The Snow Woman. When I was looking for a fairytale to bring with me to your castle, I found a piece of writing inside The Snow Woman. It was about my grandmother living here. Let's look for her there." Eiji looked up at him. They would need to search for the door that would take them into the story. One door in a sea of doors and Eiji and Sesshoshi were drowning.

"Let us find it." Sesshoshi knelt down so Eiji could hop on his back.

"You know-"

"No."

"You don't even know what I was going to say!" Eiji wrapped her arms around his neck.

"You were going to suggest we use my beast form to travel faster. The answer is no."

Eiji grumbled in a way that sounded like a low growl.

Sesshoshi chuckled. He took off, darting from door to door. The unfinished works followed them. They changed direction every time Sesshoshi did.

As Sesshoshi bounded from one door to the next, Eiji frantically scanned the titles. *Wrong, wrong.* None of the doors were right.

"Snow woman!" Eiji called as loud as she could. Sesshoshi visibly flinched from the volume of her voice. "Sorry."

The unfinished projects surrounded them now. They reached for Eiji and Sesshoshi, wandering like lost children in the white void.

"Snow woman!" Eiji shouted again.

"Do you think the door will respond?" Sesshoshi growled.

"It's worth a try. Why? Do you have any better ideas?" Eiji's attention was drawn to her left as a door knocked the unfinished works over.

The door sail toward them, opened and swallowed them whole.

Sesshoshi stumbled forward. Eiji fell from his back in his attempt to regain his balance. She landed with a thud on her side. "Ow."

Sesshoshi helped her up. "I am glad to be out of there."

"Me too." Eiji looked around. "Hopefully we're where we need to be."

Everything around her was covered in snow. They were definitely in The Snow Woman. "I didn't expect that to work." Eiji could see a few huts surrounded by the jagged snow-covered mountains that lay beyond the village. Eiji felt like a spec in comparison to the mountains. *Sesshoshi would lose me in an instant.*

"We're in the right place."

"What is this story about?" Sesshoshi looked at her. Eiji remembered how much she had loved talking about the fairytales the first time they were in this world. It was the only time Sesshoshi wouldn't take his eyes off her.

"This is a story about a lumberjack, Minokichi and his

father Mokichi. Minokichi and Mokichi go hunting after a heavy snowfall. They ventured deep into the mountains, but they couldn't find any animals. They kept looking until they were so deep into the wilderness that it was impossible to get home. A storm set in and they sought shelter at a lumberjack's cabin. In the cabin, they settled down to sleep. Minokichi awoke in the middle of the night, freezing. While he was awake he saw a woman hovering over his father. She blew on him until he froze to death. She approached Minokichi next and chose to spare him as long as he never spoke of her for the rest of his life at the risk of death. The next morning Minokichi found his father frozen to death. He stayed at the cabin and lived a solitary, silent life."

"The end?"

"Nope! When the next winter came, there was a knock at the door. Minokichi found a beautiful woman on his front step. She said she was travelling and was lost. She asked for shelter for the night and Minokichi agreed. The woman was called Oyuki and they fell in love. They married and had five children. They were very happy together, except in summer when Oyuki often became ill. Years passed and Oyuki remained as beautiful as she'd been the day they met. One snowy night, Minokichi suddenly thought of his father and his terrible death. He told Oyuki the story and she turned on him, reminding him of the promise he'd made never to speak of it. Oyuki was the snow woman. She reminded him that if he spoke of the snow woman she would have to freeze him to death. But she couldn't do it. She loved him and their children too much so she left instead. Minokichi was heartbroken but he raised their children well. Many say the snow woman can still be heard lamenting her lost love and missing her children. The end."

"Hn. Human stories are odd."

Eiji huffed but it quickly turned into a laugh. "In a way."

"And you think your grandmother is here?"

"Yes. Well, I hope so. But I know exactly where she'd choose to live if she was here. She'll be in the lumberjack's cabin, the remotest of the remote places in all the fairytale world.

Probably in all the real world too," Eiji said.

"Why would your grandmother want to be so far away from everything?"

"Yamamachi never treated us well. My grandmother loved stories. The way she spoke about them made it sound as if the fairytale world was as real. Which turned out to be true, but no one knew that and everyone thought she was odd," Eiji said. "I know she'd want the quiet of the mountains. Where no one would bother her and she could just watch nature."

"I see," Sesshoshi said. His gaze turned to the snow-covered mountains. "Let us find out who we are in this story."

Eiji saw a cabin a little ways away. *We must be in Minokichi's village.* Eiji trudged through the snow, the cold burned and froze her shins. *Ow.* She didn't have to walk much farther before Sesshoshi picked her up and carried her. He held her high above the snow as he walked through it as if it were nothing. *Stupid yōkai abilities.*

"Are you not grateful?"

"How do you always know what I'm thinking?"

"Your face reads like a scroll."

"Well your face reads like a stone."

Sesshoshi glared down at her. "I will drop you." Eiji grinned and the corners of Sesshoshi's lips twitched. "Tell me again how you have missed me, little priestess."

"No. It'll do your ego no good."

They reached Minokichi's cabin and went inside. Eiji saw an old man huddled around a fire in the middle of the room. *That must be Minokichi's father.*

"Ah, Minokichi, you have returned," the old man looked up, right at Eiji. His face was wrinkled and kind. A thick moustache covered his upper lip. Eiji could hardly see the tip of his nose.

"It's me again," Eiji said to Sesshoshi.

"Hn."

Mokichi titled his head.

"We're visitors to your world. We're looking for

someone," Eiji said.

"Ah, visitors. We don't get many of those. Well except the one that lives here all the time."

"I knew it." Eiji's heart skipped heavily in her chest. "Do you know her name?"

"Tsuru. The old woman who lives by the lumberjack cabin." Mokichi wiped his hand along his thick moustache. "We visit her every loop."

Before you die. Eiji cringed.

"You found her." Sesshoshi placed his clawed hand on her shoulder. Eiji turned and looked up at him. His golden eyes pulled her in.

"I'm going to see her again," Eiji said. The sting of unshed tears filled her eyes. Sesshoshi only nodded. The look he gave her was careful. *He's worried I won't be able to leave her.* Eiji was worried about that too.

Mokichi cleared his throat. "We can head up there now. It's time." Eiji nodded. She began to follow Mokichi into the snow when Sesshoshi scooped her up again.

Mokichi's eyebrows rose high on his face. Eiji could see his eyes now.

"My companion is carrying me. You can't see him."

"Apparently so." Mokichi turned back toward the mountains. Sesshoshi and Eiji followed Mokichi into the mountains.

They walked for hours through the snow. *I'm sure I've seen that rock before.* Everything started to look the same. Rocky and snowy with more rocks and more snow.

"You are so quiet," Sesshoshi said.

"I thought you liked silence and only silence. Humans talk to much." Eiji leaned her head against his chest. *At least I'm warm.*

"I did, until I met you," Sesshoshi said. "But humans do talk too much. In general."

Eiji smiled. "I'm just thinking."

"About your grandmother?"

"Yeah."

"Do you think it is good for the living to see the dead once again?"

"I- I don't know." Eiji frowned. "Are you worried?"

"You know I am."

"I'll be able to leave her." An arrow of dread shot through her heart. That was enough to frighten her. *I can leave her. I've lost her once before. I can handle it again.*

"We'll see."

"We will."

"Aren't I getting heavy?"

Sesshoshi let out a noise. He sounded almost indignant. "No, little priestess." His grip around her thigh tightened.

Sesshoshi put her down once they arrived at the lumberjack's cabin several hours later. The cabin was a simple log structure, covered in a blanket of snow. Behind the cabin lay another cabin of similar design. Eiji's heart beat faster. *Grandmother.*

"Did you build this for her?" Eiji asked Mokichi.

"I did."

"Thank you."

"It was a small kindness. I deserve no thanks." Mokichi glanced back at them before entering the lumberjack's cabin.

"We need to sleep in the lumberjack's cabin in order for the snow woman to come and kill Mokichi." Eiji wondered what it was like for the characters in these stories to know they'll die every cycle. *Maybe it's not so bad if you know you're coming back.*

"Alright. We can retire once we visit your grandmother," Sesshoshi said.

Eiji stiffened. "Yeah." Where was this feeling coming from? Her hesitation.

"You are afraid."

"I -"

"There is nothing to worry about." Sesshoshi took her hand and guided her toward the cabin. Eiji watched Sesshoshi pull the vines away from the front door with his clawed fingers. Snow fell from the leaves. Sesshoshi pushed the door open and dragged Eiji inside behind him.

Tsuru looked up from her spot in front of a fire.

She looked at Eiji and Eiji stared back at her. "Grandmother."

Tsuru smiled. "Eiji." She rose and embraced Eiji.

Hot tears ran down her cheeks. "I've missed you so much."

"I know. Lord Sesshoshi told me I was dead in your world. I'm sorry I didn't come find you last time you were in this world, but I thought it best. I *still* think it best, but this time it seems you have found me." Tsuru let go of Eiji enough for her to take a step back.

Eiji gave a small smile. "You might be right, but we needed to find you. I need your help. The Shogun and the Emperor have built a weapon that kills yōkai instantly and we need a way to destroy it."

"And how can I help destroy it? You should know that I can't leave this world."

Eiji clenched her fists. "Train me. Train me so I can use my reiki to destroy it."

60

Chapter 8

Tsuru tilted her head to the side. "Train you? In what way exactly?"

"The weapon seems to have some kind of foundation in reiki. It feels like I can undo it if I knew how, like untying a rope," Eiji said.

Sesshoshi watched the thoughts run through Tsuru's head. She was as open as Eiji with her expressions. He had noticed it last time they met, but it was comical now with Eiji and Tsuru standing face to face.

"I have some things I can teach you, though I don't know if it will be effective," Tsuru said. "I haven't seen the weapon, but I can show you something that could work. The rest will be up to you."

Eiji glanced at Sesshoshi. "Good." She gave a nod. *Always so determined, Eiji.* Sesshoshi found himself tense since they entered the cabin. He knew it stemmed from Eiji's emotions. He felt how hard she fought her sorrow, how difficult it was for her to remain composed. He wanted to comfort her, to pull her into his arms and lick the side of her face. He knew Eiji would not find it odd. She knew it was a way wolf yōkai comforted each other. Lord Ko had done it to her before.

Sesshoshi refrained.

Tsuru sighed. "You look tired, Eiji." Eiji's eyes filled with tears once again but they did not fall. Tsuru placed her hand over her granddaughter's. "Let us retire for the night. We can start training tomorrow. I'll be the one to visit you tonight. I'm the snow woman in this story."

That made him pause. "Permanently?" Sesshoshi asked.

"Yes."

"Oh," Eiji said.

"She's still around, the snow woman." Tsuru said with a

62

small smile on her face.

"How strange. I never thought about what happens to the characters when we take their place," Eiji said in a voice so quiet even Sesshoshi struggled to hear her.

"Let us rest," Sesshoshi said. He extended his hand and pulled Eiji up.

"I'll go freeze Mokichi now. Then you can rest all night," Tsuru said. Tsuru left ahead of them.

Sesshoshi led Eiji back to the lumberjack's cabin. Tsuru was already ducking out of the cabin by the time they reached the front door.

"Good night," she said. Sesshoshi found Mokichi asleep in the centre of the room. He was covered in ice. Sesshoshi turned back to Eiji. He took in the look on her face.

He grabbed her wrist and pulled her one step closer to him. Eiji stumbled into his chest. He slid his hand along her jaw and into her hair. He held her closer as he met her lips. Eiji seemed frozen at first as he kissed her, then she relaxed in his embrace. Tears ran down her cheeks and onto his wrist.

He pulled back and looked down at her. She bowed her head and fell into his chest. Eiji's whole body shook in his grasp.

Sesshoshi licked the trail of her tears. It startled her enough to stop her crying. Then she was laughing.

"I thought only children did that," Eiji said.

"No, it is a wolf yōkai thing, though children are more quick to give out affection," Sesshoshi said. Eiji's smile took a weight off his chest.

She took a deep breath. "Sorry, I- the visit was good. It was nice to see my grandmother again. It just hurts so much sometimes that I've lost her. And then to hear her say the same things she always did-" Eiji trailed off.

"I understand."

"Do you though?" Eiji looked skeptical. Sesshoshi could not blame her.

"Let us get some rest," Sesshoshi said. Eiji settled down on the floor of the hut. Sesshoshi curled along her body behind her. He snaked his arm around her waist and pulled her close. "I cannot wait to get proper alone time with you." He nuzzled his nose into the crook of her neck and inhaled her scent. Eiji's whole body shivered at his words. "Without a corpse nearby."

Eiji huffed a laugh. "Me either."

"Good night."

"Night."

Eiji fell asleep quickly. Sesshoshi felt her breathing even out and her whole body relaxed against him.

He closed his eyes and slept until a chill in the air woke him.

The room seemed to glow with ice. Eiji shivered in his arms. She woke and pressed back against him. Sesshoshi looked at Mokichi. He was still frozen, but someone hovered over him.

Eiji opened her mouth to speak but Sesshoshi clapped his hand over her mouth. "Shhhh. Someone is here."

Eiji seemed to see the figure then. Sesshoshi felt her mouth close under his palm. The two of them watched the figure blow a blanket of ice over Mokichi. It only froze him more. *Why? Tsuru said she was the snow woman and she already fulfilled the task of freezing Mokichi.*

"It's the snow woman," Eiji whispered. "The real one."

Sesshoshi looked closer. The figure's purple hair floated behind her like water in a river. Her skin looked like it was made of ice. When she turned toward them, Sesshoshi saw crystallized patterns in her pale blue eyes.

He could see why humans feared her. There was something ghostly about her. She was different from both humans and yōkai. The yōkai in other stories had been oddly coloured and misshapen. They looked more like children's renditions of yōkai than anything resembling real life. The snow woman was different.

The snow woman knelt before Eiji. The malice in her eyes made Sesshoshi growl and tighten his grip on Eiji.

The snow woman flicked her eyes up and looked right at him.

64

Characters in the stories were not suppose to be able to see outsiders, yet the snow woman looked right into his eyes. She stared for a moment before returning her gaze to Eiji.

"You are young. The fire of life burns beautifully in you. I have decided not to take it from you, however you must never speak of this day to anyone. The instant you do, your life will be frozen," the snow woman said.

She is behaving as if she is still a character in the story. But Tsuru has taken her role.

Sesshoshi watched the woman disappear like falling snow. He tightened his grip around Eiji.

"What was she doing here? I thought if my grandmother had taken her role she would not appear," Eiji said.

"Perhaps we know less about the fairytale world than we think."

"That's very likely." Eiji settled back down to sleep. Sesshoshi found it hard to relax back onto the futon.

"What's troubling you?"

"She looked right at me."

"Hm." Eiji was nearly asleep again. Sesshoshi lay awake for a long while afterwards until finally he slept.

The next morning Sesshoshi woke before Eiji. He removed Mokichi's body so it would not upset her when she woke.

When he returned to the cabin, Eiji was up. She looked at the place Mokichi's body had occupied. "Thank you for doing that." She shivered in a way that scrunched up her nose. "Poor guy. It's so cold."

"Let's go warm up by your grandmother's fire."

Eiji perked up. "Great idea." Together they headed over to Tsuru's hut. It was much warmer than the lumberjack's cabin. Tsuru greeted them with a warm smile. "Good morning."

"Morning," Eiji said.

Sesshoshi sat down next to the fire. He accepted the tea Tsuru offered him. Her wrinkled hand brushed his. Eiji's cheeks seemed to grow red from the action.

Sesshoshi smirked. "What is it?"

"No- nothing!" Eiji squeaked. She eyed her grandmother.

"Oh, just tell him."

"I will not."

"Fine then I will. What's he going to do? I'm already dead." Tsuru poured some tea for Eiji and settled back on her heels. "When I was alive, I thought you were very handsome."

"I am."

Eiji slapped his arm.

"I thought it would be so nice to hold your hand just once, but I knew I'd lose my head before I got anywhere close." Tsuru sighed. "But a girl can dream."

"You weren't a girl when you were dreaming of those things," Eiji scolded.

"Oh well, now my granddaughter gets to live out my girlish fantasy."

Eiji blushed from the base of her neck to the tips of her ears. "Grandma!"

Tsuru laughed.

"Hn. How amusing you both are."

"Stop looking at me like that, Sesshoshi."

"Don't be such a prude Eiji. I raised you to be more adventurous than that."

"Arg!" Eiji sipped her tea, trying to hide behind it. "Grandmother, we saw the snow woman last night. The real one. Do you know what that could mean?"

Tsuru tilted her head. "No. I see her all the time."

"Oh," Eiji said.

"How long have you been living here?" Sesshoshi asked.

"Thousands of cycles."

"Then the snow woman would have been without a role for a long time," Eiji said.

Tsuru frowned. "I never thought about it like that."

"Maybe it affects the characters differently than if we visit for just one cycle," Eiji said.

"Perhaps." Sesshoshi could tell Tsuru had never given it much thought, but it troubled her greatly now. They were silent for many moments until their tea was finished and breakfast eaten.

Tsuru finally looked ready to get down to business. "Eiji, tell me how I can train you." Eiji sat up straighter.

"You say that this weapon is woven with reiki, like you could undo it if you knew how?"

"Yes. It felt pieced together. Like there is something at the centre holding it all together and if I undid that the whole thing would fall part," Eiji said. "At least I hope it will. Either that or I could just blast it with all I've got."

"That is something we can try. If only once. And with your yōkai Lord as far from here as possible," Tsuru said. "But I think it would be best to focus on the finer control of your reiki. Then, if you find the thread within the canon holding it all together, you can pull it apart."

Sesshoshi listened. He could move to the farthest side of the story world in order to be away from Eiji's powers, but a part of him longed to feel it. Reiki was an opposing force to yōkai, one meant to destroy the other. Reiki often burned in a pleasant way when it was being equally matched. That feeling was likely what drew him to Eiji in the first place. The predatory side of Sesshoshi longed to spar with Eiji's reiki. Maybe he would get to one day, but for now he was resigned to experience it from a distance.

"We'll work on threading your reiki first," Tsuru said. "I never taught you that when I was alive." Eiji nodded.

"I will leave you to it," Sesshoshi said. Eiji looked at him with longing. "Do not miss me while I am gone, little priestess."

Eiji glared. "Arrogant yōkai."

"What will you do while we train, Lord Sesshoshi?" Tsuru asked.

"I will train as well. In the woods."

"Have fun." Tsuru smiled.

Sesshoshi left the women and headed into the woods. He could feel Eiji's reiki building already.

He found a clearing deep in the woods and worked through the mantras he had taught Eiji during their last visit to the fairytale world. When he was finished, he cut through trees with his yōkai blades. Then he chased after beasts in the forest. When he caught them, he killed them.

It was nearly midday when Sesshoshi felt sated.

He turned to head back to Eiji and found the snow woman standing behind him.

I did not sense her.

"Get out of the way," Sesshoshi said. She stared at him, but said nothing. Perhaps she really could not see him and was here by coincidence. Sesshoshi began to walk past her.

"Why are you here?" her icy voice stopped him.

Sesshoshi looked down at her. Her skin was blue. Her white hair floated behind her as if caught in the wind. "I am here with a visitor to this tale," Sesshoshi said.

"I know. Will you stay like the old woman?"

"No."

"Good. She keeps me from my love." The snow woman turned her crystal eyes to the horizon.

"Eiji?"

"No. The old woman. Tsuru."

"So you cannot take your place again until she leaves."

"Exactly."

"Normally other characters cannot see me if I am not part of the story."

The snow woman still did not look at him directly. "I see all. Are you not afraid?"

"I fear nothing."

The snow woman smiled in a way that was not kind. "That is a lie. You fear losing your Minokichi. Interesting. You fear losing her to death. You also fear that she will leave you. She has once before."

"Eiji is flighty if she feels conflicted." Sesshoshi would not ask how the snow woman knew that. It seemed to him a dangerous road of questioning to go down.

"You know her so well."

"You know Minokichi well too. Yet you choose to leave him."

The snow woman glared. "I am bound to the story."

"Not entirely or you would not be able to see me," Sesshoshi said.

"He broke the rules."

"Sometimes rules must be broken." Sesshoshi resumed walking back to Eiji.

"Then tell me, what rules did you break for her?"

Sesshoshi paused mid step before continuing.

"All of them."

Chapter 9

Eiji lay on the floor. "I'm exhausted."

"As you should be," her grandmother said. "You're doing well."

"I feel like I haven't made any progress." Eiji stared up at the blackened ceiling.

"I'll make you use your reiki on Lord Sesshoshi and then you'll see just how much progress you've made," her grandmother said.

"Not if I can't get up." Eiji tilted her head to the side when Sesshoshi entered her grandmother's hut.

"The snow woman came to see me in the mountains," Sesshoshi said.

Eiji frowned. "That shouldn't be possible."

"Tsuru, have you heard of such a thing?" Sesshoshi asked.

Tsuru shook her head. "I've never seen a character act outside the bounds of the story."

"What did she want?" Eiji asked.

"She told me that Tsuru's presence keeps her away from Minokichi." Sesshoshi frowned. "I cannot sense her. She... snuck up on me."

Eiji let out a short laugh.

"She was behind me. It surprised me to find her there."

"That's a normal feeling for us humans," Eiji said. She exchanged a smile with her grandmother.

Tsuru sighed. "I am troubled that my presence here has displaced her more than I ever would have thought. She has never mentioned it to me before."

"Does it matter?" Eiji asked. She saw Sesshoshi's eyes widen a fraction.

"I love these tales. All of them. I got so much joy from reading them myself and from sharing them with you," Tsuru said. "I do not want to disturb them."

"The snow woman leaves Minokichi anyway. Does it really matter so much to her?" Eiji said.

"I believe it does," Sesshoshi said. "How goes your training?"

"Good. Watch." Eiji gave him a tired smile.

Tsuru raised her hands and called forth her reiki. Her power surged forward and Eiji's reiki rose up to block it. Eiji fought with it to stay down until she could tap into the finer control she'd been practising.

Eiji brought out a thread of reiki from the centre of her palm. She wound it around the sharp corners of Tsuru's reiki and undid each link. Eiji had undone half of Tsuru's weave when her reiki slipped and crashed into her grandmother's. Their power sparked between them and threw both of them back.

Eiji panted. Her hands hurt. When she brought them to her face she could see they were burnt. "I slipped."

Tsuru smiled. "It's your first day. You've done well."

Eiji fell back onto the floor again. "I can't do any more today. I'm totally drained. Good thing I have more time to practice."

"It is growing dark," Sesshoshi said. "Let us retire for the night." Eiji nodded. Her head felt heavy when she did, like it would throw her off balance.

"Good night you two," Tsuru said. Eiji lugged herself up and walked with Sesshoshi back to the lumberjack's cabin. Eiji piled the remaining firewood on top of the ash from the previous night. Eiji and Sesshoshi used sparks from battling their reiki and yōkai to light the fire.

Eiji collapsed next to the fire. "I feel as heavy as a stone."

"Using reiki is difficult for priestesses."

"Is it the same for yōkai?"

"No."

"Of course." Eiji smiled. A small smirk played on Sesshoshi's lips.

"The hour is late," he said. Sesshoshi reached forward and

touched the pad of his thumb to the curve of her cheek. "You should sleep." He settled down next to her. Eiji turned and traced the strong ridges of his face.

His claws found their way into her hair. The feel of them against her scalp was one of her favourite things. Eiji pulled him down to her. Their foreheads touched briefly, his lashes descending as he breathed her in.

"Eiji."

Her lips brushed against his. There was no sense of urgency. No one was watching. No one was waiting for them. Closing the small distance between them, Sesshoshi kissed her slowly

The only need she felt was to be closer to him. Sesshoshi slipped his fingers beneath the collar of her hakuri. They shrugged out of their layers. Eiji's hands only left his skin to bare her own. They groaned together as his unclothed chest fit to hers.

Sesshoshi moved away from her lips and continued a trail down her throat, her breasts, her stomach and thighs.

"Sesshoshi" Eiji breathed as her bliss overcame her in waves. "Oh, Sesshoshi."

The rock of her hips carried him over, the pulse of her release resonating with his own. He kissed her as they rode out their pleasure together. It was easy to fall asleep after. Eiji promised never to deny herself this kind of love, this kind of pleasure, ever again.

Eiji awoke in the middle of the night to a knock on the door. She pulled herself away from Sesshoshi's warmth and went to the door. Her grandmother stood outside. She told Eiji she needed to do this to progress the story forward. "This is the part where the snow woman comes to stay with Minokichi, but I can stay in my own cabin." Eiji nodded. Her grandmother left and Eiji went back to bed.

Moments later there was another knock on the door. Eiji frowned. Had her grandmother forgotten something?

The cold wind bit her cheeks when she opened the door.

The snow woman stared back at her.

"I am a traveller. I've lost my way and I'm distressed. Won't you give me shelter for one night?" The snow woman said. One word floated through Eiji's mind. *Manipulative.* Eiji hadn't had much attachment to this story when her grandmother read it to her when she was a child, but now the tale felt sinister.

"We've already done this part of the story," Eiji said. The snow woman only stared at her. "Come in." She stepped back from the door. Sesshoshi was awake now. He sat up and looked at the snow woman. It was obvious she stared back.

"You know we're guests here," Eiji said. The snow woman nodded. Eiji turned to Sesshoshi. "Can we make her sleep outside?"

"Eiji, I have never heard harsher words leave your mouth." Sesshoshi looked almost proud.

The snow woman hissed. "This is my home." She pushed her way by Eiji to settle herself inside.

Eiji exchanged a glance with Sesshoshi.

"It's your home, but my grandmother occupies your place. What has that done to you?" Eiji asked.

"I am stuck in between. I cannot live with my love," the snow woman said.

"You leave him anyway," Eiji said.

"I have to."

Eiji huffed. She sensed this line of questioning would get her nowhere. "Why have you never asked my grandmother to leave before?"

"I-" The snow woman started but she never finished. The silence stretched on. Eiji looked away from her. "It's late. We'll talk in the morning." The snow woman lay down far from the fire and turned her back on them. Eiji settled back down to sleep as well.

The next morning, Eiji sat cross legged in front of her grandmother. Her eyes were closed. Eiji focused on the reiki around her. Her aura flitted back and forth as she thought of the snow woman.

"You're distracted," her grandmother said.

Eiji opened her eyes. "I just... the snow woman came last night. She tried to fill her role in the story."

"Ah."

"She said that since you occupy her role she can't live her life with Minokichi. She's stuck in a void. Sort of. I think," Eiji said. She watched her grandmother's face as Tsuru took in what Eiji was saying.

Tsuru frowned. "I didn't realize. She never told me." The shine of unshed tears filled her grandmother's eyes. "I never wanted to displace the characters. She's always been here... I didn't think..."

"It's ok," Eiji said.

"It's not. I love these stories, all of them. And all of the characters have a place in my heart."

"But she just leaves him. The snow woman leaves Minokichi."

Tsuru shook her head. "That is her choice. You might not agree with it, but that decision is not the sum of her character. I think she would like to stay, but that's not how the story is written."

"What will you do?" Eiji asked.

"I should leave. We'll finish your training and then I'll go."

"And live where?"

Tsuru went still. "You're right."

"About what?" Dread settled in Eiji's stomach.

"When I first met Lord Sesshoshi I had been living in the Overworld. I created a kind of portal for myself so I could hop from story to story, and stay in my own world in between. But I became lonely. The Overworld is so hostile. I decided to settle somewhere permanently. I chose The Snow Woman when I was alive and that was still where I wanted to go," Tsuru said. "I can't go back to the Overworld. Living there is not a life. And I cannot stay here knowing that I have pushed the snow woman out of a home."

"So what then?" Eiji bit her lip. This conversation wasn't going anywhere that she would like to follow.

"I don't know yet." Tsuru looked away. *She's deflecting.* "I'll let you know when I've figured it out. Right now I just need time to think."

"OK." Eiji relaxed back into her seat and closed her eyes. She'd give her grandmother the time she needed to think, but she wouldn't let this go completely.

Eiji refocused on her reiki. She wove it in strands through Tsuru's reiki. Her control was improving. This was the feeling she was after. The first time the weapon fired, Eiji felt the reiki to her core. It was unstable, held together by something fragile that could be undone if someone could only get close to it.

They trained all morning until Eiji requested a break. "I'm so tired."

"Reiki pulls much out of the soul," Tsuru said.

"Do you still feel it?"

"No. Not really. Not like when I was alive."

"Ah," Eiji said. She stood up and stretched. Her joints popped and her muscles ached. "We can train after lunch again. If that's alright."

"Of course," Tsuru said. Eiji nodded and headed outside.

Eiji found Sesshoshi in the middle of the gardens. He stood and watched the fields. Eiji came up beside him and intertwined her fingers with his. The corners of Sesshoshi's lips quirked up.

"What?"

"Human displays of affection are odd."

"Says the yōkai who licks people's faces to comfort them." Eiji smiled. She watched the fields too. "Are you making sure the crops don't cause any trouble?"

Sesshoshi scoffed. "Do humans never stand and think?"

"Hmm, not really. We talk to think... I think."

"That explains a lot."

Eiji squeezed his hand. "I told my grandmother about the

snow woman."

"What did she say?"

"I don't think she knew, or realized, what her place in the story was doing to the snow woman," Eiji said.

"What will she do?"

Eiji ran her bottom lip between her teeth. "She said she needed time to think."

"But you know what she will choose."

"I'm afraid she'll destroy herself so she no longer lives in the fairytale world at all," Eiji said. It was hard for her to say it out loud. It had crossed her mind the moment she'd told her grandmother. *She loves these stories too much to let any character suffer. She'll leave if she can't find a way to stay that isn't disruptive.*

"Will you try and stop her?"

Eiji sighed. "I don't know." Eiji knew, logically, that her real grandmother was already dead. She'd grieved, mourned, said her eternal farewell, but this version of Tsuru was so life like, so real.

Sesshoshi ran his clawed finger along the back of her hand. "I am confident that you will make the right choice when the time comes."

"I hope so."

Chapter 10

Eiji trained again in the afternoon and Sesshoshi stayed outside. Her reiki itched against his skin, but he could not stay away.

"Lord Sesshoshi?" Tsuru's voice drew his attention.

"What is it?"

"I believe Eiji is ready to unleash her full power."

"Ah. I will move away." Sesshoshi moved from the hut and found the place in the story where the map looped back on itself. It was the same as when they had discovered it in The Tale of the Bamboo Cutter. The landscape suddenly finished where it had started. This would be the farthest possible distance away from Eiji.

The tips of his ears felt cold. "Why do you follow me?" Sesshoshi knew the snow woman was near. He was learning how to detect her.

"I fear Eiji will destroy me as well."

"You are not yōkai."

"I do not know what I am, but her power might be enough to undo me."

"You will regenerate when the story starts over."

"I do not think so."

Sesshoshi quirked a brow. *If it is true, that is different from the other stories.* He waited for her to say more.

"I've watched this story start over every time. I do not wake up anew like Minokichi does. Like I use to," the snow woman said.

Sesshoshi could feel Eiji's power building from where he stood. Reiki rippled through the woods like a drop in a pond. A wave of air crashed through the forest, bending the trees and blowing his hair back. He had never felt a power so strong within a human priestess before.

"What is it you wish from me?" Sesshoshi asked the snow woman when the forest had settled.

"I want that woman to leave so that I can take my place in my story again." The snow woman's hair floated around her like a coursing river.

"Why ask me and not Eiji?"

"Her attachment to her grandmother is clear. If Tsuru must leave for me to stay I do not trust Eiji will do what I ask of her."

"You are more observant than I have given you credit," Sesshoshi said. "But I hope you are wrong. Eiji and her grandmother love fairytales. They would not want you to suffer."

"We shall see. Her being here changes everything, even the flow of time itself."

Sesshoshi said nothing to the snow woman before leaping into the trees and returning to the lumberjack's cabin. He could feel Eiji sleeping inside. *She feels... thin.* Sesshoshi's lips curved downward.

Tsuru sat with her. Sesshoshi made his way over to them and settled down beside Eiji.

"She did very well," Tsuru said.

"She is strong."

"You are probably ready to return home once she's rested," Tsuru said.

"And what will you do?"

Tsuru gave him that smile, the same one from when they first met. Like she knew more than she let on. "I'll do what I know I must and you must help Eiji deal with that."

Sesshoshi nodded. "I understand." He scooped up his intended and carried her back to their temporary hut so she could rest in his arms.

A few hours passed before Sesshoshi felt her breathing change. He watched Eiji's eyes flutter open. She smiled at the sight of him.

"How long was I asleep for?" Eiji yawned and stretched against him.

"A few hours."

"Well, that confirms it. That kind of blast of reiki isn't practical. It'll knock me out," Eiji said.

Sesshoshi nodded. "It is often best to use ones power carefully rather than recklessly."

"Did you feel it?"

"Hn, yes."

Eiji's cheeks grew warm.

"The snow woman spoke with me while I waited for you to finish with your training," Sesshoshi said.

"Oh? She seems to like you. What did she say?"

"She is indeed stuck in this world without a place. You're grandmother occupies her spot and she cannot live in the story as she should."

Eiji sat up, a frown on her face. "And it bothers her?"

"Of course. Why would it not?"

"Well, she leaves him. Minokichi. I always wondered why she didn't change the rules. Like, if she loved Minokichi, and the only person he told was actually the snow woman herself... after so many years of keeping it secret... then why didn't she just stay with him? Who would know that she'd gone back on her own word."

"You are asking how she did not manage to talk herself out of an irrational decision based on the evidence and experience before her? Really, little priestess?" Sesshoshi gave her a look.

Eiji opened and closed her mouth a few times before responding. "That was different."

"Was it?"

"Oh, shut it."

Sesshoshi's smirked was triumphant.

Eiji looked at the ground. "I'll have to tell her."

"Tsuru?"

"Yes."

"I told her. She will not stay here." Sesshoshi smelled the salt of Eiji's tears right away.

"She'll tell me to destroy whatever ties her to this world. She said it herself. She can't live in the Overworld and she can't live in a story without displacing a character," Eiji said.

"She is already gone."

"I know."

Sesshoshi cupped the side of her face and ran his clawed fingers through her hair. "I know it is difficult for you even if I cannot understand it."

"Thanks." Eiji leaned into his touch.

Sesshoshi helped her up and together they went to speak with Tsuru. Sesshoshi stood back as Eiji spoke. He watched her gestures and her face more than listened to her words. He knew what she would say already.

"Eiji you must," Tsuru was saying.

"I know, but..." Eiji's bottom lip quivered.

Tsuru sighed. "I wish your yōkai Lord had never told you about me. I understand why. You needed my help, but now you must destroy the piece of writing inside The Snow Woman's scroll.

Eiji's eyes widened. "That's what keeps you here?"

"I didn't know if it would work when I was alive, but I wrote a small story about myself. What kind of memories and powers I would have, all that stuff. I figured if this is the world where all things created lived, then if I created myself in writing I would appear here too."

"Very clever," Sesshoshi said.

"Thanks. That piece of writing is all that allows me to stay here. It makes you feel like I'm alive, but I'm not."

"Aren't you?" Eiji's voice was desperate.

Tsuru tilted her head. "No. I feel like I did when I was alive, but I also know I am not. I never feared death, Eiji. I'm not here because I'm running from it. You had a hard time letting me go at home too. You're repeating the feeling."

"I-" Eiji started, but she stopped.

"We will do it together," Sesshoshi said.

"But then I'll really never see you again," Eiji cried. "Forever this time."

Tsuru touched her granddaughter's shoulder. "I know. It is

the burden the living must bear. And you cannot start a new life with the one you love by living in the past." Tsuru flicked her gaze to Sesshoshi.

Eiji wiped her tears away and nodded. "I know. I'll do it."

"You should go Eiji. You are ready and you shouldn't stay any longer."

Sesshoshi came up beside Eiji and laced her fingers with his. It felt strange to initiate, but he knew it would mean more to Eiji than a lick on her cheek.

Eiji took a shaky breath. Sesshoshi felt her body tremble through their linked hands.

"Alright," Eiji said. Eiji finished the story. She told her grandmother she remembered the snow woman and her grandmother vowed to leave. Eiji hugged her grandmother tight, crying into her kimono sleeve.

The portal to the Overworld opened behind the lumberjack's hut. Sesshoshi felt Eiji's fingers find his again. They went to the portal. Eiji turned to look back and Sesshoshi glanced back as well. His attention was drawn to the snow woman. She stood a ways behind Eiji's grandmother. She watched them, her icy eyes were piercing even from afar.

He gave her one last look before he passed through the portal with Eiji in tow.

Back in the Overworld once again, Sesshoshi's eyes took a while to adjust to the brightness.

He looked down at Eiji. She seemed to shrink into his side.

"Are you alright?" he asked.

"Yeah. I'll be OK," Eiji replied. He watched her muster her best smile. "If the tori gate is far we could travel on your beast for-" Eiji stopped. Sesshoshi was relieved to see the giant red tori gate that marked the way back to the real world close by. Eiji looked disappointed.

"Aw-"

"We can just walk." Sesshoshi smirked.

He lifted Eiji and they raced toward the gate.

84

They made it to the tori gate and Sesshoshi leapt through it.

86

Chapter 11

They were back.

Eiji pulled away from the cursed scroll and sat back on her heels. Sesshoshi sat next to her, looking more out of sorts than usual. It was the feeling of being pulled back into the real world. - discombobulated.

Eiji turned and dug through the pile of scrolls.

"Are you going to do it now?" Sesshoshi asked.

"Yes, before I lose my nerve." Eiji found The Snow Woman and unrolled it. Inside Eiji found the short scroll with her grandmother's handwriting. She didn't reread it. Her whole body shook. Eiji forced her reiki forward. The scroll turned to ash. The pieces fluttered to the ground around her.

"I am proud of you." She felt Sesshoshi's hand on her shoulder.

She closed her eyes tightly. "That was horrible."

"It was what was right," Sesshoshi said. She glanced at him then. His golden eyes gave her comfort. "We should have time to show the Shogun that we can destroy the weapon before he decides to march on the north."

"I hope he will see reason and ally with us."

"And what will Lord Ryuu do then?"

"I do not know but I hope it will end in less blood shed than a full war will."

"I thought yōkai liked killing."

Sesshoshi tilted his head. "In a way, yes, but we do not like a mindless slaughter. You should know that by now."

Eiji frowned. "I do."

She heard her father come through the fabric flap that hung over the back door. The sound was so familiar it made her smile and sigh at the same time.

"Father has just returned. We must have been gone no

more than an hour," Eiji said.

"Hn."

"Father. We're here. I don't want to frighten you," Eiji called.

"We?"

Her father came around the corner and froze. The colour drained from his face before he dropped to his knees. He placed his hands on the ground and rested his forehead on the tops of his hands. "Lord Sesshoshi. Our home is not worthy of your presence."

"You may rise. The home of my intended is always worthy."

A shiver ran through Eiji's body. The look on her father's face made Eiji worry he might faint.

"Y- your intended?" Hiroki's voice cracked.

"It's a recent development," Eiji said.

"His intended!" Haruka burst through the shōji screen. Her claws cut through the paper. "I'll fix that. Eiji! Hello again Lord Sesshoshi, I am but so humbled in your presence, blah blah blah."

"Haruka!"

"You promised me an explanation a week ago and now to appear out of nowhere and drop this news?" Haruka's face hadn't relaxed since she'd entered the room. "I'm so happy for you, but what the hell, girl!"

"Fair," Eiji said. "Let me make some tea and I'll explain it to you both." She glanced at Sesshoshi and saw no resistance from him so she moved everyone to the kitchen. Eiji made tea and set down the clay cups in front of Haruka and her father. She explained about the scroll, their first time in the fairytale world and this last visit. She left out the more intimate details, though the look on Haruka's face told Eiji she'd already filled in the blanks. Eiji also left out finding her grandmother during either of their visits.

"Mother wasn't crazy," her father whispered. Eiji knew how he felt. The look on his face reflected her own feelings from months before.

When Eiji looked over at Sesshoshi she saw he looked concerned. "What's bothering you?"

"Haruka said we have been gone a week. That cannot be right. Last time we were gone mere moments."

"We think we were. We don't know for sure."

"No, but the scribe was sent the same day I came to Yamamachi. It would not have been more than a few hours."

"We've been gone for too long. But why?"

Sesshoshi growled. "The snow woman said that her displacement in the world affected everything, even time itself. It must have had something to do with that." Sesshoshi talked around Tsuru as if they'd never seen her. Eiji sensed he didn't want to raise more questions from Eiji's father and Haruka. Eiji would tell them about it when she was ready and when they had more time to spare. They'd lost too much already.

There was a shift in the air.

Sesshoshi raised his head. "Something is happening. In the North. It no doubt has something to do with Lord Ryuu."

"And the weapon," Eiji said. Her stomach dropped to her feet. She thought they'd have more time.

"We must go."

"I'll come with you," Haruka said. For a brief moment she remembered her place. "If Lord Sesshoshi does not mind." Eiji was so proud of her.

"Do as you wish."

"That's not a no! Let's go." Haruka exited the house through the hole she'd made.

Eiji followed Sesshoshi out the proper front door.

His jaw was tight and his fists clenched. "I fear we do not have much time."

"Which means..." Eiji could only hope.

"I will use my beast form to travel with you."

"Yes! It's happening!"

Sesshoshi gave her a stern look that made her reign in her enthusiasm. "Eiji, I have told you before, raw yōkai is dangerous. I do not make this decision lightly."

"Still *so* excited," Eiji pushed out through clenched teeth as she tried not to smile. "I'll keep you in check with my reiki." That seemed to appease him.

"See that you do." Sesshoshi moved away from her until he was clear of the village. Eiji watched as his body became engulfed in a white light. The shape of it swirled and there was more and then less of him until the light started to grow. Eiji shielded her eyes. Haruka leapt to her side and clutched her arm. "Half breeds can't do this. We don't have enough yōkai to change."

"It's really something." Eiji didn't take her squinted eyes off Sesshoshi as he transformed into something like a wolf. His paws could easily crush her and he wouldn't feel it, like stepping on a pebble. His white fur was unruly, so unlike the yōkai lord himself.

The light dissipated when his transformation was complete. Sesshoshi turned his large head to look at her. His eyes were blood red. Eiji thought she saw no recognition in them, like he didn't know who she was. He'd never looked at her so coldly, not even the first time they'd met.

He turned and padded over to Eiji and Haruka. He put his snout down to their level. On his exhale, Eiji's hair blew back.

"Your breath stinks, my Lord," Haruka said.

"Haruka, you're going to get yourself killed."

"I think he appreciates honesty. Seems like that's why he fell for you."

Eiji paused. She had been pretty blunt with him since the beginning. *It was the fairytale world that allowed me to do so.* Sesshoshi lowered himself to the ground and Eiji took that as a sign to climb on his back. She used his fur to pull herself up until she sat in the centre of his shoulders. *I'm not dead and Sesshoshi seems to be in control of his yōkai. This is really cool!*

Sesshoshi growled beneath her.

"Sorry. I'll stop getting excited about your potential doom."

Haruka waved from below. "I'll follow you. Something

tells me that climbing onto his back will be that step too far that I'm trying to avoid."

"Ok!" Eiji yelped as Sesshoshi took off. She gripped onto his fur and ducked down as far as she could. The landscape below her moved like a rushing river. She couldn't make out anything they passed.

They arrived in the north to find the land in turmoil. From her perch on Sesshoshi's shoulders, Eiji could see the Shogun's samurai marching toward the northern palace. They were specs in the distance, but Eiji could make out the shape of the weapon among them.

She felt it too. The reiki within it sparred and sparked. *It's so volatile. So unstable.*

The northern palace made Eiji's stomach churn. She was too far away to make out the details, but it looked as if the palace grounds and walls were smeared with blood. There were darker flecks and chunks all over the ground. Eiji didn't want to imagine what they were.

"Sesshoshi, I'm sure you can smell it, the northern palace is bathed in blood," Eiji said. *Maybe Lord Ryuu killed all the humans on his lands like he said he would. Or maybe this was just from one battle.*

Sesshoshi lowered to the ground and Eiji slid off his back. She stepped back into the cover between the trees and waited for Sesshoshi to transform back into himself again. His body started to glow but then stopped. He snarled and growled. The glow emerged again but faded out a moment later. He growled again. It looked like he was fighting himself. *This is what he was afraid of.*

Sesshoshi fought harder. His large paws landed close by and crushed a bunch of ferns. Eiji retreated further into the woods. Sesshoshi's thrashing grew more erratic. Eiji found herself running from his movements. His claws landed in front of her. *That was close.* Eiji turned to run the other way. Sesshoshi didn't see her. His red eyes looked far away as he thrashed and snarled.

Eiji ran farther away but Sesshoshi always moved closer. One of his steps equalled twenty of hers. Eiji yelped as she tripped over a root. She looked up to see Sesshoshi's paw coming toward her. She rolled away, but it wasn't far enough.

Her body was swept up and out of the way.

Eiji looked up to see Haruka dragging her.

"Thanks."

"I got you, girl." Haruka grinned. "We need to take him down."

Eiji shook her head. "I don't think he needs aggression right now."

Haruka shrugged. "You're his *intended*. You know best." It was obvious by the tone of Haruka's voice that she was still annoyed with Eiji. Haruka sighed in her dramatic way. "Intended. I'll never forgive you for keeping this from me."

"That's fair. Now boost me up."

Haruka grabbed Eiji around the waist and leapt into the air. She threw Eiji onto Sesshoshi's back. Eiji grabbed a fist full of his fur and held on. Her arms burned as she struggled to maintain her grip while he thrashed. Eiji dug through his fur until she found his skin. She placed her palm on him and pushed a calming wave of reiki into him. Using reiki like this worked for those who were sick, ailing or anxious, but Eiji wasn't sure of the effect it would have on yōkai.

Sesshoshi stilled under her touch. His breathing came in heavy. Eiji held her breath. Then he glowed white and started to shrink. Eiji yelped as she fell to the ground. She figured Haruka would catch her like always, but the closer she got to hitting the forest floor the more worried she became.

She landed in Sesshoshi's arms instead. He looked down at her with his golden eyes. He set her on her feet and gave her only a moment to get her balance before pulling her to him for a kiss. Eiji could hear Haruka squealing behind her, but she was easy to ignore.

Sesshoshi's kiss told her more than she'd ever heard him say.

"Thank you," he said when he pulled back. "Do you now understand why I do not like to use my yōkai form? It is not transforming that is the hard part, it is reigning the yōkai back in."

Eiji nodded. "I understand. I don't want to see you fight yourself like that again."

Sesshoshi sniffed the air. "We must go and see how the north fairs." Eiji followed Sesshoshi and Haruka toward the northern castle. As they got closer, Eiji saw the humans marching toward the castle, the weapon in tow. They were close now.

"My father is over there." Sesshoshi pointed to the opposite side of the castle from where the humans approached. They moved towards the western soldiers.

"Do you think your father is here to help Lord Ryuu," Eiji asked.

"It is not likely. He would side with the Shogun."

"The west isn't known for getting involved in the affairs of others. And Lord Ryuu is particularly hateful of humans. The north and the west don't mesh," Haruka said.

"There are hardly any western soldiers. My father has likely come to talk Lord Ryuu out of whatever he is thinking of doing. Or halt what is already underway," Sesshoshi said. Eiji could tell it bothered him deeply to be so out of the loop. *We weren't suppose to be gone for this long.*

Sesshoshi forged ahead. Haruka and Eiji fell behind a little. Eiji had no doubt Haruka could keep up with Sesshoshi but she likely wanted to stay close to Eiji.

"When Katsu and I get engaged I'm not going to tell you for years," Haruka said.

"Fair." Eiji pushed the thin branch of a tree away from her face. "But you can't keep a secret to save your life."

Haruka made a disbelieving noise that let Eiji know she was right.

As they got closer, the more clear the charred shapes on the horizon became. Eiji saw the bodies of humans and yokai strewn across the hills. During their time in the fairytale world Lord Ryuu and the Shogun had begun warring. *Such devastation already.*

Eiji and Haruka followed Sesshoshi until he found his

father.

"Father, what has Lord Ryuu done?" Sesshoshi asked. Lord Jou looked surprised to see him.

"Sesshoshi, where have you been. You've been gone for days."

Eiji and Sesshoshi locked eyes. "We had only meant to be away for a few hours but we were delayed by... a snow woman."

"A snow woman?"

"She was an abnormality," Sesshoshi said.

"What are you talking about, son?"

"It no longer matters," Sesshoshi returned his gaze to his father. "Tell me what has happened."

"Lord Ryuu slaughtered every human within his boarders and the Shogun told him to stop or face the weapon. Guess what Lord Ryuu chose? The weapon takes time to transport so the Shogun sent soldiers to die in the meantime." Lord Jou looked out at the horizon with sadness in his eyes. "I came here to change his mind, to get him to ask for forgiveness, but he will not see reason. I have given up."

"Are you returning to the western lands?" Sesshoshi asked.

"Yes. There is no hope to be found here."

"I can destroy the weapon." Eiji spoke with confidence though she didn't feel it. Lord Jou's gaze suddenly made her shrink. "At least... I think I can."

Lord Jou regarded her with a careful look. "Even if you can, then what? Lord Ryuu will slaughter the humans."

"Not if we help them," Sesshoshi said. "This is the type of opportunity you have been waiting for. If Eiji destroys the weapon and you help the Shogun defeat Lord Ryuu, that will improve relations with the humans."

Sesshoshi's father tilted his head. "The idea has merit."

An energy rose within Eiji's chest.

The weapon is charging.

Everyone turned toward where the humans advanced on the northern castle. Eiji watched a pink glow fill the canon and then fire across the landscape. Every yōkai in its path was wiped clean from the battle field.

"Father, we cannot let the Shogun possess a weapon like this. We can form an alliance with them if they want protection from yōkai, but this weapon is the path to the destruction of our kind," Sesshoshi said.

Lord Jou sighed. "Even if your human can destroy the weapon they will build another." Eiji bristled at his reference to her. *People have called Sesshoshi "your yōkai" before and you liked it,* Eiji reminded herself.

"Eiji will destroy every weapon they make. And she may be able to train other priestesses to do the same."

"Then she will be assassinated."

"She will be protected."

"By who?"

Sesshoshi grabbed Eiji's wrist and pulled her to his side. "By me. When she is mate."

Lord Jou's eyes widened. Lord Jou's features settled into a look that Eiji recognized as resolve. It was only because she knew Sesshoshi's expressions so well that she could read his face. "This really is the dawning of a new age." Lord Jou looked at the weapon once again. "And it will be, whether or not we are successful."

"Father, gather the western army to aid the Shogun. I will speak with him and Eiji will destroy the weapon."

"How will she get close enough?" Lord Jou asked.

"I'll take her," Haruka spoke up.

Eiji looked at her best friend. "It's too dangerous Haruka." Eiji's eyes burned with unshed tears.

"It's too dangerous to go alone. I'll protect you," Haruka said.

"You will keep her safe." Sesshoshi said it like a command.

Haruka took a deep breath just for show. Eiji felt a speech coming and rolled her eyes at her friend.

"In the limited time you've been in my company, almost

everything I've said has been enough for a Lord to kill me. Let me continue the trend." Haruka levelled her gaze on Sesshoshi and his father. "You may love Eiji now, but I have loved her since she was a child. I have never met a person as loving and kind hearted as her. I want us to raise our future children together, side by side, as sisters. If you think I will let anything happen to her then you know nothing of love."

Eiji sniffled. "Haruka, don't be so dramatic. Let's go." Her voice wavered. She pulled Haruka along by the arm. Haruka's gaze lingered on the two yōkai lords for a little longer. She looked like she would pounce on them if they even looked like they disagreed.

Eiji caught Sesshoshi's eye and she gave him a pointed look. *Be careful.*

Once they were a ways away from the two lords Eiji let go of Haruka's arm. "That was quite the speech."

"It wasn't all theatrics you know. I can be serious too."

"I know and I'm so grateful to have a friend like you."

"And yet you hid your secret love for the western lord," Haruka said.

"Yeah, yeah." Eiji and Haruka ran through the forest together. "Let's destroy the weapon so you and Katsu can live in peace and we really can raise our children together."

"Your half-yōkai babies are going to be so cute," Haruka said. "I can teach them everything there is to know about being confused by your bloodline."

"As long as you keep the theatrics to a minimum," Eiji said.

Her attention turned to the weapon. She could see it clearly now. The canon-like structure stood smoking at the crest of the ridge. She would need to wait until it fired again to try and destroy it. That would mean staring death in the face and hoping she survived.

98

Chapter 12

Sesshoshi watched his father speed off toward the west and Eiji retreat into the forest with Haruka in the east.

Sesshoshi darted across the battle field to where the Shogun stood with his weapon. Sesshoshi tried to avoid conflict with either side, but it could not be helped. A human samurai lunged when Sesshoshi landed too close. Sesshoshi cut him down. A yōkai soldier from the northern army aimed his arrow at Sesshoshi. He sent out his yōkai blades and sliced the northern yōkai into three.

The battle field was slick with blood. *This fight seems so pointless. It is like Lord Ryuu knows he can slaughter the humans and so he does. And the Shogun knows he can kill yōkai with his weapon and so he does. All they are doing are losing their own men.* Yōkai fought with purpose and honour. Lord Ryuu had clearly lost all his sense.

Sesshoshi leapt over the Shogun's guards and landed before him. "This must end."

"Tell that to Lord Ryuu. He started this whole mess," the Shogun said. He squared his shoulders. "He slaughtered all the humans within his lands. He keeps us from getting medicinal herbs that we need. This is *his* doing."

"Your weapon only encouraged him."

"Your kind has been destroying us for centuries!"

"I am aware. I came here to offer the aid of the west, if you destroy your weapon."

The Shogun looked outraged. "Absolutely not."

"Then we will destroy it for you," Sesshoshi said. "And we will destroy the north."

"That is war."

"So is this." Sesshoshi inclined his head to the scene behind him.

"The weapon cannot be destroyed. It is held together with reiki. Yōkai cannot go near it," the Shogun said.

"A human could."

"A human would not dare. This weapon is the only defence we have against your kind." The Shogun stuck out his jaw. "A human would never destroy our only means of protection."

"An alliance with the west would offer you protection," Sesshoshi said.

"I only need my weapon. I will not trust any yōkai after all they have done to us."

"We will see." Sesshoshi turned and headed back to the forest. He hoped to catch up with Eiji and offer her more protection as she approached the weapon.

A presence within the forest made him slop.

"Lord Sesshoshi," Lord Ryuu's voice stopped him in his tracks. "How nice of you to join us. You smell like your human whore. Has she kept you away?"

There were times that Sesshoshi wished he were as reactive as Eiji. His claws itched for Lord Ryuu's blood, but that was not the way yōkai emotions worked. Emotions flowed through yōkai like a sieve, it didn't fill up and spill over like it did in humans.

"Eiji is none of your concern. You are slaughtering every human that resides within your domain. Edo is not only for yōkai," Sesshoshi said. "It takes only a simple mind to see that."

"It takes a simple mind to see how quickly the humans have become like us as soon as they have the means," Lord Ryuu growled. "They will kill us all to get revenge for the years yōkai have slaughtered them."

"So you both kill each other? To what end?"

"It does not matter to me as long as there are no humans left on my land." Lord Ryuu laughed in a way that consumed his whole chest. "You are so young Lord Sesshoshi and you are foolish like your father. It is also easy to see how your love for that human has clouded your mind."

"I have never seen so clearly," Sesshoshi said. "Do not think yourself victorious already Lord Ryuu. You might not live past the end of the day."

Lord Ryuu's smirk twisted his face in an ugly way. "Be happy I do not take your words as a threat, pup. I vow to be free of all humans that place their dirty feet on my lands." Lord Ryuu looked off into the distance. "And by the looks of it, your whore is trespassing."

Sesshoshi snarled. "To kill the intended of another land is to declare war on them. Is that what you wish?"

Lord Ryuu stilled. "Your *intended?* Is the depravity of the west so deep? Then I will not mind destroying you and your family once and for all." His eyes stayed on Eiji. "And she will be the first."

That was enough for Sesshoshi to strike him without any consequences to his father's rule. He lunged, claws ready, only to be pushed back by Lord Ryuu's yōkai. He began to transform into his true yōkai form and Sesshoshi could not touch him. Lord Ryuu grew into a black beast with broken claws and fur that clumped together in patches. *I must transform as well.* Sesshoshi's frown was deep. Letting his yōkai loose twice in one day was dangerous. Especially considering the fight he had had with his beast earlier. Eiji had been the one to break him free of it. *She did it once, she can do it again.* At his current size, Sesshoshi would have trouble fighting Lord Ryuu. The beast could reach Eiji faster than he could. Sesshoshi had no other choice.

Sesshoshi let his yōkai loose. His paws touched the ground and he shook out his fur.

Lord Ryuu bounded toward the battle field and Sesshoshi grabbed him by the tail with his jaws.

Lord Ryuu yelped. His giant paws slid backward in the dirt until he found his footing. His claws sunk into the ground and Sesshoshi struggled to pull him any farther. Lord Ryuu swung around and batted Sesshoshi in the face. His hold on Lord Ryuu's tail slipped as he reeled back. His cheek stung. He felt warm blood run down his face and drip onto his white paws.

Lord Ryuu moved toward the battle field again. Sesshoshi leapt after him. He landed on Lord Ryuu's back. Sesshoshi aimed to bite his neck but Lord Ryuu managed to shake him off.

Lord Ryuu kept attempting to advance toward the battle field. Sesshoshi pulled him back. He growled at the northern Lord.

You will get to Eiji over my dead body.

Lord Ryuu growled back. The message was clear.

That can be arranged, pup.

Chapter 13

The ground rumbled and Eiji swung around to look behind her. Two huge wolves barrelled toward her. *Sesshoshi!* Her heart raced and sank at the same time. He was back in his yōkai form. He'd struggled so much to regain control not long ago. He would have to do it again.

Who's that in front of him? Eiji guessed it was Lord Ryuu. The beast headed right for her.

The weapon drew her attention in the other direction. She felt it spark and come alive. It would fire soon. It aimed at Sesshoshi and the other yōkai. *It'll kill them both.*

"Haruka! We need to stop the weapon. It'll destroy Sesshoshi," Eiji called. Haruka finished disposing of a human samurai that had stood in their way.

"Right," Haruka said. She grabbed Eiji and hoisted her onto her back. They travelled across the battle torn landscape. Eiji's eyes watered from the speed. She wondered if Sesshoshi had had a chance to speak with the Shogun. She hadn't sensed him moving in that direction, but she'd been distracted by staying alive.

A yelp behind her made Eiji turn in her perch on Haruka's back.

"Eiji stay still!" Haruka hissed.

"Sorry." Eiji saw a glimpse of the beast's jaws leaving Sesshoshi's paw. Blood stained his white fur red. Eiji looked away just as Sesshoshi pinned the other yōkai.

The weapon was ready. Eiji whipped her head around.

"Drop me here and get out of the way," Eiji said. She leapt from Haruka's hold and stumbled forward.

"Eiji!"

"Go!" Eiji felt the burn of tears at the corner of her eyes. "I can't lose you. Get away from the weapon." The conflict was clear on Haruka's face. "Go!"

Haruka bit her bottom lip. Eiji worried she would insist on staying, but then Haruka turned and left without arguing. *No theatrics. This is killing her.*

Eiji ran toward the weapon. It glowed pink at the centre. One of the yōkai howled behind her. *I know you're stronger than him Sesshoshi.* Eiji had to believe he would win or else she wouldn't be able to focus on the weapon. She only knew how to destroy it in theory. She needed all her concentration to make sure she could destroy it in practice.

The weapon fired. Eiji fell in front of it, catching the blast a second before it would have continued on to Sesshoshi.

The shot of reiki hit her. Her limbs felt like they would rip from her body. Eiji's reiki pushed out to defend her. She controlled it into a solid burst that pushed back at the canon's wave. Her skin felt too hot. Every nerve in her body told her to run, move away from the blast, but Eiji held her reiki steady.

Once her feet were firmly planted on the ground, she straighten herself against the blast. Eiji focused on the things her grandmother taught her. The reiki from the weapon ebbed and flowed. There was a path to it, a road that Eiji could follow to find the place where it weaken.

She couldn't hear anything distinct around her. The reiki rushed by her ears like a raging river. The glow of it blinded her. Eiji felt cut off from all her senses and yet more connected than she'd ever been.

There was a spot at the centre of the canon. A place no human or yōkai would be able to touch while the weapon was in action. Eiji could reach it. Or at least she could try. She focused most of her energy on protecting herself. Eiji separated a thin strand of reiki to penetrate the centre of the canon. Her reiki snaked around in the centre, pulling the canon's reiki tight. *I have to choke it out.*

Eiji felt fatigue heavy in her arms, but she persisted. She had to or it would be her death. Her body burned. She focused only on binding the canon's reiki.

There!

Eiji pulled her reiki tight and snapped the canon's reiki. The reiki inside the canon came apart and pushed out. The body of the canon shattered into tiny pieces. Shards grazed her cheek and drew blood.

Eiji fell to the ground when the canon's reiki no longer pushed against her. The force of it knocked her flat on her back. She gasped for air. She should see the sky, but all she saw was white. *I'm blind.* Cold panic rushed through her. *Sesshoshi. I need you.*

Eiji was exhausted and unable to see. She'd been so willing to push Sesshoshi away when she was strong, but in this moment she realized how much she needed him. Always. *When I'm happy or sad or scared or feeling powerful I want him there.*

"I'm such an idiot," Eiji said.

"I could have told you that." It was Haruka's voice. She was somewhere beside Eiji and yet Eiji had no sense of where. The whiteness surrounded her.

There was a growl, a snarl and then a whimper somewhere behind her. Then silence. Eiji could feel Sesshoshi's yōkai strong and steady behind her. It wasn't him that was dead, it was the other yōkai. Eiji felt relieved and frustrated at the same time. She wanted to see him.

"Eiji, can you stand?" Haruka asked.

"I think so." Eiji hauled herself up on shaking legs.

Sesshoshi's yōkai began to rage and Eiji turned toward him. She stumbled over her own feet and Haruka steadied her by gripping her shoulders.

"I can't see."

"You what?"

"I'm blind. It's only temporary. I think."

"Let's hope so. Eiji, Lord Sesshoshi's in trouble."

"I can feel it."

"I can see it," Haruka said. "I've seen this before. Though only once. Lord Sesshoshi is fighting with his yōkai and it isn't letting him go."

"What happened the last time you saw this?" Eiji asked though she was sure she already knew the answer wouldn't be good.

"The yōkai drowned himself after fighting for three days to change back."

Eiji's stomach dropped. "Do yōkai really hate their own nature so much?"

"This isn't who they are anymore than that pink glow from your reiki is who you are," Haruka said.

Eiji nodded. "Take me to him."

"What? Eiji, he's thrashing around." Eiji knew. She could feel the ground quake. "He'll crush you either by accident or on purpose."

"I brought him back last time. I can do it again."

"You can't get close to him."

Haruka was right. Maybe Eiji could use her reiki to weave her way closer to Sesshoshi just like she had with the canon. "I don't need to be close, just close enough. Please Haruka."

"Fine." Eiji felt Haruka's arm loop around her waist and she was pulled forward. Haruka bounded with Eiji in her grasp until she landed and let her go. The ground shook more forcefully here and Eiji could feel Sesshoshi's yōkai more strongly.

"This is as close as I'm letting you get," Haruka said.

"Thank you. Now I need you to leave me here so I can use my reiki without hurting you."

"You're asking a lot of me today," Haruka said. There was a bite to her tone.

"I know. Last request, I promise."

"Don't get smushed," Haruka said before Eiji felt her yōkai move away. Eiji wasn't sure what was around her. Bodies? Swords laying on the ground or poking out of corpses? Wood? She needed to stay as still as possible.

In the white of her sight she could somehow see Sesshoshi fighting. The outline of his yōkai formed in her vision. Eiji stretched out what was left of her reiki toward him. His yōkai fought her off, batting away her attempts to reach him as if she was no more than a cicada.

Eiji split her reiki into several tendrils. She let them dance around his yōkai, some distracting and some sparring. It was challenging keeping track of them all. Some of her reiki strands disintegrated when she couldn't maintain her focus. *Just a little closer.* Eiji wove her way around Sesshoshi's yōkai until her reiki caressed the side of his face. She heard a growl, low but subdued.

Eiji held her reiki steady against him. She felt the ground shake as Sesshoshi approached her. *He's not going to hurt me.*

The feel of his yōkai told her he was right in front of her. Eiji reached for him and expected to feel fur. Instead his clawed fingers slipped between hers and Eiji felt his lips against her own. Her eyes went wide for only a moment before closing. Tears ran down her cheeks.

"I'm so glad. So, so glad." She kept repeating it.

"I know, my love," Sesshoshi said. He pulled her into his arms and threaded his fingers through her hair.

"How do you manage to make even that sound arrogant?" Eiji grumbled. Sesshoshi chuckled. Eiji's world faded from white to black as she slid into Sesshoshi's embrace.

Chapter 14

His father was pacing. Lord Jou began to wear on Sesshoshi's nerves.

Lord Jou stopped for a moment. "You know you can leave her for a little while. Just to attended to some of your duties."

"Pass."

"You cannot deny your father."

"I will put up a fight if you try and make me leave Eiji's side."

"You are no better than a love struck pup."

"Perhaps, but this love struck pup won you an alliance with the entire human race. I would say you owe me at least this." Sesshoshi tracked his fathers movements. Back and forth. Back and forth.

His father stopped. "Fine."

"Excellent. We do not need to have this conversation every morning. My answer will remain the same until she wakes." Sesshoshi moved his gaze from his father to Eiji. She still slept after four days. He had been told not to worry. That had not stopped him.

"She does this when she's used too much reiki," Haruka had told him. "Don't worry. She'll wake up when she's ready to kick ass again."

His father left the room and Sesshoshi was alone with Eiji once again. Sesshoshi had stayed by her side since she fell into his arms on the battle field. He carried her past Lord Ryuu's body and to where his father, the western army, and the shogun with his men awaited them. Haruka had followed close behind him the entire time.

The Shogun had bowed to Sesshoshi then. "I thought you were full of shallow promises. I have never seen a yōkai embrace a human like that before. Perhaps it is time for our kind to unite with yours." Sesshoshi had felt the shift in Haruka's emotions. He understood why. Eiji once told him of Haruka's parents and their love for each other. It had gone unnoticed by so many.

"Then you have not been looking close enough," Sesshoshi said. Haruka relaxed and that was the end of it. Sessoshi left his father to discuss the details of an alliance. As it stood now, humans would not make another weapon and the western army would keep human villages safe from any yōkai that thought to go on a killing spree.

Since then Sesshoshi's focused was Eiji's well being.

Eiji gasped violently and shot upright. Her whole body buzzed with reiki. Sesshoshi reached for her and steadied her shoulders. Her skin burned his palms as the purifying reiki washed over it. It felt good.

"Eiji, it is alright,"

Even her eyes glowed pink. Her breathing evened out. The reiki retreated back into her body. She looked at him. He watched her eyes settle back into their rich brown colour. "Sesshoshi."

He pulled her into his arms and held her tight. "Eiji. You slept a long time."

He felt her nod against his shoulder. "That's common when I use too much reiki. I really had nothing left. I don't think I've ever overdone it so much before."

Sesshoshi pulled back to look her over again, as if he had not been staring at her for days already. "Is that all it was?"

"Yeah. I'm fine. I can feel it. My reiki is stable again. I'm good, really." She looked worried now. "What happened after I fell asleep?" Eiji asked. Sesshoshi told her about the alliance and Lord Ryuu.

"You killed him."

"He threatened you."

"Oh yes, a perfectly fine reason to kill him then."

Sesshoshi smirked despite her chastising tone. "It was."

"You yōkai are so blood thirsty."

"You knew that already, little priestess."

Eiji shrugged. "So, what can I use to wipe your memory

this time?" Sesshoshi growled. "What? Too soon?"

"I have no intention of ever letting you go again."

"I can live with that."

Sesshoshi peered down at her. "When will we have have our mating ceremony?"

Eiji blushed all the way to the tips of her ears. "I – um - I don't really want to be paraded around all of Edo as the new mate of Regent Death himself. I don't think I could handle that many people staring at me."

"Oh, you mean for a shinto wedding ceremony?" Sesshoshi said.

"Yes. What do yōkai do?" Eiji quirked a brow.

"Yōkai mating ceremonies are private and very.... physical."

"Why am I not surprised." Eiji smiled. "I don't want a ceremony. Not the way it would be done for the mate of the western lands, but I do want something just with my father and Haruka."

"That can be arranged."

Eiji smiled wide.

"Eiji!" Lord Ko crashed through the shōji screen and leapt into her arms. He knocked her over. She laughed and smiled. Sesshoshi grabbed Ko by the back of his robe and hoisted him off of her. "Be gentle."

Ko found his way back into Eiji's arms a moment later. "I was so afraid. I'm glad you're OK. Big brother wouldn't let anyone near you."

"Oh really?"

"Yes! He was moody and protective and-" Ko was silenced by a growl.

"You'll have to tell me more when he's not around," Eiji whispered into Ko's ear. Sesshoshi heard it easily. There was a mischievous glint in her eye.

"For now you must let Eiji rest."

Lord Ko pouted, but did as he was told.

Eiji lay back on the futon. "I think I'll just rest my eyes for a bit."

Sesshoshi listened to her breathing even out. He pulled the blankets up to her shoulders and settled back down at her side. They would have time to plan their union once Eiji was fully recovered. For now Sesshoshi was content to rest by her side.

A week later, they gathered at the spot of Eiji's grandmother's memorial. Eiji's father preformed the ceremony between Sesshoshi and Eiji. Haruka cried and Katsu, her intended, stood tall and proud while an aura of *please don't kill me Lord Sesshoshi* radiated off of him. Sesshoshi found his fear amusing.

There had been a time where all Sesshoshi had to entertain him was the distress of others. Not anymore.

He looked down at Eiji. She was strikingly beautiful in her white kimono. He was glad she had wanted to have a small ceremony just so he could see her like this. It would not be long before her hands would be covered in dirt again, before she smelled like herbal concoctions, before she was ruffled from playing with Ko. Sesshoshi had found all of it repulsive when they first met and now these were things that seemed so part of her very being that he could do nothing but love them.

The words of the snow woman drifted through his mind.

Which rules did you break for her?

All of them.

Author's note

Thank you for reading! I hope you enjoyed it. Thank you to amazon users Maria and Tiffany. My goal with my first ever self-published novel was to sell it to one non-family/friend and you two were it! Not only that, you left such kind reviews. I'm so glad you enjoyed the first book and I hope you like the second.

Welcome to new readers. I hope you enjoyed the world I built and the characters.

If you find any errors in this book and wish to report them, please email lindseymerril@gmail.com.